Fatima's Room

Fatima's Room

Charlotte S. Gray

Arc Light Books
Portland, Oregon

Fatima's Room

Gray, Charlotte, 1944—
Fatima's Room / Charlotte Schiander Gray
ISBN: 978-1-939353-25-2

Published by Arc Light Books
Portland, Oregon
www.ArcLightBooks.com

Cover and book design by Jan Camp

GLOSSARY

Allah, refers to God in Abrahamic religions

As-Salam-Alaikum, greetings of peace to you

angareeb, a wooden bed frame with a woven string surface

asma'ai, listen

diya, blood money

Eid, holiday after Ramadan

emma, lightly woven white material

fatur, the break-the-fast meal at night during the month of Ramadan fasting

ferenji, (white) foreigner

fūl, Fava bean dish, served with tomato and raw onion

girgir, arugula

haboob, sand storm

hadith, tradition in accordance to words, actions, or habits of prophet Mohammad

haram, forbidden by Islamic law

hilumur, a bitter-sweet drink for Ramadan

infibulation, the sealing of the vulva by stitching it together

jellabiya, a loose, ankle-length cloak

kakerde, hibiscus tea

kisra, fermented pancake

mabruk, wishing congratulations

mumken, maybe

Pharaonic circumcision, surgical removal of the clitoris and labia, and sealing of the vulva by stitching it together

sheikh (m.), sheikha (f.), a leader or elder in the community

souq, market place

suhoor, the morning meal

Sunna circumcision, the surgical removal of the clitoris

tabouleh, a vegetarian dish of cracked wheat, parsley, tomato and mint

talaq, I divorce you

taquiyah, small rounded skullcap

tobe, a five-to-six-meter long cloth for body and head wrapping

ulama, scholar or authority on Islamic law

yani, I mean

zar, a ceremony for exorcising evil spirits from women

For the Sudanese women who opened their hearts to me. And for women all over the world who struggle for more opportunities and a better life in dignity and recognition of who they are.

CONTENTS

one

In the afternoon the dusty roads of Khartoum stretched empty in the shimmering desert heat. Whiffs of dust rose between the beige and brown walls and powdered the big iron gates. Pressed upward the tiny dust grains disappeared into the milky blue. Suddenly the bright afternoon faded and the vault of heaven erupted in flaming layers of melting lava that quickly hardened into diamonds in the darkening sky. A small sliver of moon appeared like a curved dagger of light in the black.

Men dressed in white emerged from houses and strolled down streets. The loose sleeves of their *jellabiyas* waved in the air as they were making a point. Some may have heard a woman scream from behind one of the big metal gates, but the sound was muffled by the breezes playing in the leaves of the plane tree.

The silent night in the town by the river was barely disturbed.

In a shuttered, sweltering room a young woman lay sweating. She had just turned on the light. Her recent nightmare had been particularly vivid. The men had led her down a sandy road that ended in a gully in the desert. Her hands were tied behind her back with a rope, and she stumbled, almost falling a couple of times. When she came to the end of the road the men stood in a semicircle in front of her.

She knew she was not to resist when the men grabbed her and put her in a hole to her shoulders.

A stone hit her temple.

That's when Fatima had screamed.

Still shaking, Fatima rose from her bed and draped a shawl over her shoulders. She sat down by her small table and looked at the blank windowpanes that reflected the bare wall behind her. There was nothing. She bent over her coarse notebook and began to move her pen slowly. She had been confined to her room for days. She didn't remember how many; it was all a blur to her. Hesitantly, she wrote. *Day turns into night, turns into day. Light and dark. Yesterday, tomorrow, today. What is the difference?*

Fatima's favorite uncle had given her the notebook to help her keep track of the days. She now recorded the date of 21 December 1998. She sat a long time and then she finally ended her brief entry, *Today is first day of Ramadan. The decision will be made by the end of Ramadan.*

Fatima stared at the dark window; it was still early evening. She stood up and moved her arms. She had no feeling in them. She wiggled her fingers; it was as if they resisted bending. Her whole body felt dead, wrapped in an invisible shawl of numbness.

She bent forward and began to pray.

A little reassured, she lay down on her *angareeb*, a wooden bed frame with a woven string surface, and closed her eyes.

She opened them again to avoid the frightening faces of the men, who all looked like Uncle Hamid. Abruptly, she fell asleep.

She was awakened by Ilham, the housekeeper, who brought her *suhoor* consisting of orange juice and a little bread before dawn. She drank her juice and tried to get her bread down under the watchful glare of her dark windows.

22 Dec. The only reading I have is the Koran. I have been reading it a little.

23 Dec. Just eighteen and I have already ruined my life.

Fatima's five daily prayers helped break up the endless time. Slowly she settled into her room, the silence inter-rupted by Ilham's rattling pots in the kitchen, the voices of passing pedestrians. Her headaches gradually subsided and she grew used to her thirst. In this manner day turned into night turned into day.

The days were easier than the nights. She had trouble fall-ing asleep, and when she succeeded her nightmares returned; men dressed in white with stones in their hands. She would get up and write in her diary. *I worry what they may do to me. Will they kill me?* She would close her eyes and think of her grandmother's garden. She imagined herself back in her Paradise, crouching in her hideout between the roots of her grandmother's banyan tree close to the deep waters of the Nile. There she had felt safe.

If only grandmother was here.

On the 26th, a day exactly like the previous days, Fatima sat reading the Koran at her desk when she was startled by a knock on the door. After a brief pause, her maternal uncle, Muhammad, entered her room with two other men.

Fatima quickly covered her head with her shawl. She rose and looked down.

Her uncle, a jovial, rotund man in a crumpled jellabiya, stood next to her paternal uncle, Muhammad, her father's older brother, and a *sheikh* leader she had seen at family gatherings but had never spoken to. He was also called Muhammad; her maternal uncle almost sounded apologetic as he repeated the name.

Her paternal uncle was the oldest of the four brothers. He wore an impeccable woolen suit with a vest, and looked past Fatima's head with a stern expression. The sheikh, with a longish white beard, nodded to Fatima.

Her uncle told her to sit down, and although she sat very straight, she kept her gaze on the dusty shoes of the men.

Fatima's heart started to pound when her paternal uncle placed a briefcase on her desk right next to her open diary. But the uncle seemed entirely focused on the briefcase and its contents.

Fatima's maternal uncle cleared his throat. "Fatima, you know why we are here. I told you we were coming."

Fatima had known they were coming, but not why. She nodded her head slightly.

The paternal uncle undid the clasp on the briefcase, swung the cover back, and pulled out a long parcel wrapped in bloodstained paper. The brownish paper crackled as he meticulously unwrapped a broad kitchen knife.

"Is this the knife you used in the kitchen?" the paternal uncle held the knife high in front of her. He turned it over and for a brief instant the reflection from a piece of glass in the wall outside the window blinded Fatima.

Fatima hesitated. "Yes."

"Is this the knife you used to attack your father?" the sheikh asked.

"Yes," Fatima whispered.

"Did you tell your sisters that you were going to kill your father?"

"Yes. No.… I didn't plan to. We all said it. My father often said he would kill me.…" Fatima's voice faltered.

"We're not interested in what your father said," the paternal uncle said.

"As I mentioned to you," Fatima's uncle said after a silence, "the cause of death has not been established."

Turning towards the sheikh, her maternal uncle continued. "It is not clear if Fatima's father bled to death from the wound to his neck or if he had a heart attack. The family opposed an autopsy and went ahead with the funeral immediately. He was said to have a weak heart. His doctor can testify to that. He may have had a heart attack at the moment or around that time. We shall never know for sure."

"In other words, whether directly or indirectly, Fatima caused her father's death," the paternal uncle said curtly.

"That depends on how you see it." Fatima's uncle had black rings under his tired eyes. He addressed the sheikh. "The family didn't want the police involved. They wanted to keep this a family affair and avoid all publicity.…"

"That doesn't mean we don't seek justice," the paternal uncle interrupted.

He turned towards Fatima's maternal uncle. "You keep a sharp eye on Fatima. I hold you responsible for her while we're waiting for my younger brothers, Hamid and Arif, to come back at the end of Ramadan to make the final decision. Until then, I hold you responsible." He was sweating heavily in his woolen suit.

The three men made ready to leave the room.

The sheikh noticed the Koran on Fatima's desk. "*Allah Karim.* Allah is Generous," he said and looked at Fatima.

Fatima's uncle went over to her and kissed her on her forehead. The sheikh nodded again and the three men left.

Fatima remained in her chair. Slowly she took off her scarf and her eyes wandered to the outside wall with the glinting piece of glass across her window and up to the blue patch of sky far, far away.

After a long while she hesitantly picked up her pen. She felt surprised that she wanted to write but as she began to put down the particulars, *my uncle came with another uncle—the oldest brother of my father—and our sheikh…* it dawned on her that the interview hadn't gone very well. Fatima had wanted to explain that she had acted in self-defense when her father had grabbed her arm and pinched it so painfully, how he had beaten her so many times, how threatened she felt, how she lived in a daze of fear and dread. But how could she explain her wrath? Her red, hot fury. They wouldn't understand or they would claim a woman's anger was not to be taken seriously.

Whatever she said would be irrelevant. They had already made up their minds. Well, not her maternal uncle. He would defend her. Or would he, when he was alone with the men? She felt the three men were still standing behind her—looking over her shoulder.

She picked up her pen and wrote, *I hated my father and I wished him dead even if I didn't plan to kill him. But then I did it. It was too late.*

She dropped her pen. What difference did it make that she didn't plan to? They lived under Sharia Law. The men would retaliate. She turned and looked round her room.

They had taken away the peace of her place.

There was the same knocking on the door; again, Fatima stood up.

The sight of her dear uncle broke down her resistance and Fatima started to sob. Her uncle put his arms around her and kept them there. "Hush, hush. You'll be okay. We'll settle the matter. Hush, hush. You'll be safe with me." Fatima had always been close to her maternal uncle.

Slowly, Fatima's sobbing subsided.

"I lost my temper. My father was so bad to us. I hated him."

"I know, I know." Uncle Muhammad gently stroked her unruly hair.

"He made me do it. He..."

"Hush, hush. Allah Karim."

"But what do my paternal uncles want?"

"I'm not sure—but we'll settle. Muhammad, as the oldest and most influential, is the key. We have to settle with him; then the others will follow."

"But will Uncle Hamid settle?"

"If Muhammad does…"

"But Uncle Hamid…"

"What about Uncle Hamid?"

"Don't you think he is evil?"

"Evil? How? What do you mean?"

"I…I don't know."

"But Uncle Arif you like."

"Yes, he was always kind. As long as Aunt Awatif doesn't interfere."

"Yes, Awatif is a pain."

"You are right about that." They both smiled.

"I'll be back tomorrow. Do some writing."

Uncle Muhammad hugged Fatima and closed the door behind him.

She sat down. She still hadn't been able to tell her uncle. She had never told anybody about the time Uncle Hamid had put her on his lap behind the table so nobody could see it. Then he had touched her, touched her private parts. She was only five or thereabouts. She didn't understand but she knew it was wrong, terribly wrong. But she felt so ashamed she couldn't scream or tell him to stop, and afterwards she could tell no one. No one.

From then on she always ran away from Uncle Hamid when he approached her alone. But one more time he cornered her once she was alone in the living room. She thought she was going to die and he had talked to her just like an uncle will talk to his niece: calmly, a little humorously. But then he had grabbed her and touched her again. This time she was going to scream but she had no voice; fear had dried up her vocal cords. She must have been eight by then because she came close to telling her nice second grade teacher, Mrs. Sharma. She couldn't tell her grandmother; Fatima had wanted to keep her Paradise clean.

After that he never caught her again. He almost succeeded that one time by the river but she had torn herself loose and had run to her banyan tree and climbed high up. She had always been on the lookout.

Would he now want revenge?

two

It was the 28th of December and Fatima was following her uncle's suggestion to describe her room in her diary. The room was big and bare; the peeling walls reached to the high ceiling, its cracks and water stains filling the empty space with an imaginary landscape. The main crack down the center to the bare light bulb was the Nile. The splotches next to the Nile were her grandmother's garden and the banyan tree. This way she could lie on her angareeb and look into her grandmother's garden. This way her room opened up to the world outside.

The room had two doors: one leading into the rest of her uncle's guest house, and on the opposite wall, one opening out to the garden. The outside door had a screen on the inside. Next to that door a smallish table leaned against the wall underneath the double windows. A simple wooden chair was pushed under the table. The end wall was dominated by Fatima's angareeb. From there the brown tile floor stretched to some bamboo shelves stacked with clothes and various toiletries at the far end.

The room looked uninhabited except for the open diary and a carafe of water next to the Koran on the desk. A shawl was thrown on the angareeb. Fatima was describing her room as precisely as she could. She sat for a while, then she added, *It's the first time I have a room all to myself.*

But each lonely day seemed endless, and the nights were full of scary male faces until Ilham knocked on Fatima's door before dawn. Ilham was more regular than a clock, and her firm steps brought Fatima release from her nightmares. Dear Ilham carried the sour-sweet *hilumur* drink, freshly baked bread, and some fruit on a tray. After Ilham placed the drink and the food on the little table, she leaned over it to open the window and push the outside shutters apart to let in the sound of a predawn chirping bird. Fatima would get up from her angareeb and draw the shawl over her shoulders, listening. A message from a friend? But most enjoyable was Ilham's food; Fatima loved the sour-sweet drink hilumur and saved it till after she ate the dried figs and small bananas, all before the crack of dawn.

The taciturn Ilham kept busy with her household tasks. Fatima wanted to talk to Ilham but didn't know what to say except to thank her.

Fatima knew that Ilham came from a village outside of Sennar on the Blue Nile, south of Khartoum, and was a remote relative of Fatima's uncle. She came to work for him when his wife, Rawia, died from cancer. Her uncle had also told Fatima that Ilham had become an orphan when her father was killed in the war in Southern Sudan, and her mother died of malaria soon after.

Ilham was a devout Muslim and very critical of the present government and its use of Islam for its own ends. The other day Fatima overheard Ilham talking to her uncle in the corridor between the kitchen and her room. "It used to be enough to be a Muslim," she said. "Now there are good Muslims and bad Muslims."

Fatima searched the Koran for answers to her many questions. She read the same passages again and again. She hoped to find some reassurance about her own situation but then she was not sure it related to her. She didn't think the Koran talked about a woman. Or a daughter who killed her father. Who could imagine a daughter killing a father? It never happened.

But in Chapter Four, Murderer of a Muslim, it seemed to say that if somebody killed by mistake, not intentionally, he or she didn't go to Hell. Blood money should be paid. But "whoever kills a believer intentionally, his punishment is Hell, abiding therein; and Allah is wroth with him and He has cursed him and prepared for him a grievous chastisement."

She closed the Koran and cried.

Why did she have this life?

The hot days continued from the predawn meal till the silent Ilham appeared again with juice or *karkade* tea to break the fast after sunset. Fatima's little activities of prayers, readings of the Koran, writing and exercises filled only a small part of the long, blank day. Most of the time she sank into anxious thoughts and unhappy childhood memories. They were a family of six sisters. There was clearly a curse on them, and their distraught parents had lost hope they would ever have the coveted son. The daughters were confined to their house and to domestic duties when not in school. But even submissive, obedient daughters could never replace a son.

Fatima thought of how the days had been equally long in her own home; but in a different way. She recalled how by 5:30 in the morning her father had shouted for them to get up; once he was awake, his daughters were not allowed to sleep. And they had to whisper when he was in the house. Whenever Fatima spoke in a normal tone, her father would shout, "Fatima, lower your voice—I don't want to hear you."

Fatima made tea for him and served it on a tray in the living room. One sister tidied his room and made his bed. Another cleaned the sisters' two rooms. They were really the domestics in their house; if it hadn't been for her grandmother and aunt there would have been no school—and they would just have been married off. It was also her grandmother who had helped her get into college.

It only happened because her father was away in Saudi Arabia. Fatima and her older sister Rawia had been talking with her grandmother about going to the women's college in Omdurman, the twin town to Khartoum. Her Aunt Selma, Reem's mother, heard about their wishes and said she would help pay for it. Then Fatima could go to college with her cousin and best friend Reem, two years after Rawia.

Fatima's mother didn't see "the reason" but finally she had given in. It was good luck that Fatima's father was gone for so long or they would not have succeeded. The father was furious when he came home and said his usual, "It is not necessary." He yelled at his wife because she listened to her older sister and accused her of trying to be "popular" like Selma.

Fatima was afraid the whole thing would be canceled, but since everything was already arranged and paid for, her father let it be. But he kept yelling and told the girls not to get any silly ideas and that they had to go straight to classes and straight home and if they did not obey him, they would not be allowed to continue in school.

When Fatima started the women's college she went every morning with her three-year older sister Rawia. Rawia began her third year when Fatima started in her first. They were always in a rush to get to the bus on time.

The oldest sister, Zena, who had a secretarial job in an office of a relative, took the two youngest, Jalaa and Selma, to a primary school a few houses away. Ghada took another bus to a secondary school.

There was a six-year gap between the four older girls and the two young ones; the mother had had two miscarriages. In the mornings she stayed in bed till the sisters were out of the house. Sometimes Fatima imagined her mother used that time to pretend she didn't have all those girls.

The father was picked up by a minibus for his work. He had some kind of bureaucratic job in the government; the girls did not know exactly what he did there.

When they returned from college and schools in the afternoon heat, Fatima and her sisters cooked and served lunch for her father. He sat at the dining table, leafing through the daily newspaper. He didn't look up when Fatima entered the room with his food. He only grunted. When she put the plate in front of him, he grabbed the bread and started to shovel the food into his mouth.

Sometimes he shouted with his mouth full of food. "Fatima, bring me more rice" or "bring me more bread. Hurry up." Or, if something was not to his liking, he pushed his plate away and yelled, "Not enough sauce." The girls scurried around to please him. The mother ate alone in the kitchen before the sisters, who would have the leftovers. There was not always enough to quell their appetites.

After the meal her father watched TV till he dozed off. Sometimes the mother watched with him. Often, the father then left to go to his other wife. He had married her some years ago, before the birth of Jalaa and Selma. Fatima didn't know much about the second wife; she lived completely separately from their family. All Fatima heard was that she was very young—and very poor.

Most of the time, the mother sat in the living room and listened to the transistor radio. When she didn't listen, she locked it up so the girls couldn't use it.

They didn't need it, she said.

Books were rare. Sometimes when there was a library book or a book from a relative, their mother would hide that, too. No need for them.

Why should they read? The father joined in.

One sad memory after the other descended on Fatima. Once, she had cut corners with a kitchen job and her mother had yelled at her to redo the kitchen floor. Fatima had lost her temper and shouted back, "What for?" It was not the first time Fatima's temperament had gotten her in trouble.

Her father had happened to hear her answer. He got himself out of his afternoon couch, walked over to Fatima, and grabbed her and threw her against the wall.

Furious, Fatima had yelled, "I hate you and mother."

The father, who had been on his way out of the room, turned around and came briskly back. Leaning over his prostrate daughter, he hissed, "What did you say, Fatima?"

This time she kept quiet.

"Who asked for your love?"

He started out the room again, "We don't need your love. Nobody needs your love."

Her father had made her a nonperson—he and Uncle Hamid.

But that was long before the disaster.

There was a knock on the door. Still cringing over her unhappy memories, Fatima tried to put her face in a neutral expression and answered as calmly as possible, "Please come in."

Fatima's Uncle Muhammad peered in. "I see you are writing in your diary. How is it going?"

"So-so. But I'm beginning to like it. It's like I'm talking to somebody."

"Keep it up."

"I know. But you have to promise not to read it."

"I promise not to read it. It is for yourself."

"But I miss my sister Ghada so much," Fatima began to cry. "And my best friend, cousin Reem. And my grandmother. When will she come back from Darfur?"

"Your grandmother will be back for the holiday of *Eid*. You must have patience. We can't contact her; she is still in that remote village. She knows nothing about what happened."

"Can't you send a messenger? She is the only one who can save me."

"We have to wait till she comes back. Your father's brothers have been in telephone contact but the connections to Mecca were bad. Also they don't seem to agree on the course to take. They will definitely want to have a family meeting when they are all back together. And they will rather wait till after Ramadan now that you are safe with me here in my house."

This was her uncle's way of telling her that they still had some time, Fatima understood.

"But uncle, what do you think will happen to me?"

"Well, as you know under Sharia rules there are three options: Your paternal uncles may pardon you; they may decide to settle if your uncles on your mother's side (including me) can pay blood money; or they may want revenge."

Fatima rose abruptly and raised her hands.

"Allah Karim. Allah is Merciful." Her uncle tried to soften his last words.

"Uncle….?"

"I promise you, Fatima, that I will do everything in my power to settle this matter. Rest assured, we'll succeed. Insha'Allah. Allah willing."

"Uncle, but Uncle Hamid…."

"What is this thing with uncle Hamid?"

"I want you to talk to him. And Uncle Arif. You have to get them on your side too."

"I will talk to them when they come back. It's hopeless on the phone. Now they will soon be on their way to Indonesia. They have important business. But Muhammad is here—and as I said, he's key."

"I know; I just want you to talk to all of them."

Uncle and niece sat silently while the room seemed to grow bigger around them.

After a while, Fatima's uncle said in a lighter tone, "I will bring your sister Ghada as soon as possible—and your friend, Reem. That is if I get a little smile from you."

Fatima hugged her uncle. He moved closer to her and stroked her hair. This made her cry again. Her uncle rocked her gently and gradually her sobbing subsided. In the quiet, a branch scraped against the window.

Fatima whispered in a thick voice, "My sweet uncle. You're so kind. Even if you're a man." They both smiled. This was an old joke of theirs.

"Remember all the fun we had when Ghada and I were small and you would hide behind the banyan tree and jump on us? And we were so frightened. And you would grab us and swing us around and pretend you were going to throw us into the river." They both laughed.

"I was so afraid of the river after Aunt Selma's little Muhammad drowned."

"Yes, you were scared but that didn't stop you and you naughty girls hid my shoes. You climbed high in the tree and left them there and when it got dark you couldn't crawl up so high again, so finally Jalaa had to get them down. She was the smallest and could scale those branches like a squirrel."

"I want to see Jalaa, too," Fatima's eyes were filling again.

"Sure. Jalaa too."

Fatima closed the door gently behind her uncle. She knew he was so worried about her. He looked tired with those puffy pouches under his eyes. Fatima knew he was also thinking about her mother, his sister Amani. And he still mourned the loss of his wife, Rawia, who had died several years ago. He had not remarried, though you are supposed to in Sudan. Celibacy was not acceptable; there was great pressure to marry a younger sister or other female relative of the deceased wife. Fatima thought his resistance showed how much her uncle had loved Rawia. It proved you could have a marriage with love. She would only marry for love herself. She had discussed this with her uncle, who believed that arranged marriage could lead to a love marriage. That was true about her Aunt Selma but that was another time. Fatima felt differently.

Maybe Ilham would make my uncle a good wife, Fatima suddenly thought, when Ilham brought her food before the next morning. It occurred to her that her uncle seemed to linger when Ilham was around; and she looked in no hurry either. Fatima confided these observations to her diary during her midday writing time.

three

$\mathcal{H}$er uncle kept his word, and in the afternoon Fatima was woken from her afternoon nap by Ghada running into her room. They embraced and hugged and cried and laughed. Ghada, who was fifteen, pulled a small package from under her blouse.

"This is from Jalaa, she wanted me to bring it."

Fatima unwrapped the gift, and a banyan tree branch with green leaves and a couple of dried up reddish fruits appeared on the crinkled silver foil. Fatima touched the cherry-like rough fruits on the branch lightly and ran her hand over the smooth leaves and along their sharp edges.

"My sweet sister." They hugged again and Ghada reported how the sisters stood united. Whatever happened, they would defend Fatima. Ghada's exact message from the sisters was "Not to lose courage; they would find a way." Ghada spoke slowly and clearly, but she didn't look convincing to Fatima. And what about her older sister Rawia, who was still angry with her?

"I can only stay with you very briefly now. It's a secret from mother, uncle brought me here," Ghada almost whispered. With a sad face Ghada continued, "We are discussing what to do to help you. We have asked to see the sheikh to make him intervene; we realize it is hopeless with our paternal uncle. He doesn't think we are anything. We want to explain to the sheikh about our unhappy home life and tell him what a wonderful sister and person you are. How you have always been an obedient daughter." Ghada's eyes were getting blurred. "But we haven't received an answer yet. Jalaa also offered to travel to Darfur to get grandmother. We advised her against it; it's too dangerous. You know her, she is feisty. But we agreed it would only get us into more trouble, so we'll just have to wait for grandmother. And she will come. But you know Jalaa—I shouldn't be surprised if she hatches a plan on her own. Or if she's suddenly gone on a secret mission." Ghada hesitated. "But time is running out." Her little sister looked scared.

"But you know Uncle Muhammad has told me he will arrange a settlement with blood money. You know uncle, he keeps his word." Fatima smiled encouragingly at her sister just as her uncle returned to bring Ghada back to her homework and house chores. Ghada put on a hopeful face as she embraced Fatima one last time.

After her sister left, Fatima's smile faded. Ghada had tried her best, but her obvious lack of confidence had only increased Fatima's forebodings.

Ghada looked so vulnerable. Her visit made Fatima remember the time when they were both circumcised. Memories she preferred to suppress but at this moment she could not hold back the painful images.

The two older sisters had been circumcised before Fatima and Ghada. All they knew was that it was called the *Pharaonic*. They had heard that *Sunna* was to be preferred. They didn't know that the Sunna version consisted in removal of the clitoris in contrast to the Pharaonic one, which cut away just about everything before the wound was sown together. They had heard about infibulation but the exact details were hazy to them.

They were circumcised, two daughters at a time, and three times over the years. Fatima was to go with her little six-year-old sister. Fatima was nine. But she remembered it like it was yesterday. The women of the family had told them they would be given money, henna, and new dresses, and that they would be celebrated and wished *mabruk,* congratulations.

How cheated they had felt, she and her sisters. No one had explained to them what it was all about. They had been tricked.

She had heard from her older sisters, that it was very bad and very hard. She was afraid and told her mother, she didn't "need" it. Then her mother had shouted at her older sisters, ordering them to say nothing about circumcision.

One day early in the morning they had walked to the doctor's clinic, she and her sister and her grandmother on her father's side. It was just a few streets down in an ordinary house that was also the doctor's residence. Their mother didn't go with them. They didn't know why.

The doctor and his assistant took her sister first. They had said, "You have more courage than your sister. You are not going to shout or scream." Later they had said, "You are older, it's a shame, if you scream. You will not cry, Fatima."

But the terrified Ghada, who had been told nothing about what was going to be done to her, had shouted. She yelled and screamed. Fatima was on the other side of the door, listening. She had never been more scared; she was sobbing when they took her into the doctor's room. She immediately saw a table with little knives and scissors and gauze. She cried even harder. First they gave her an injection; the grandmother was holding her arms and the attendant her legs. She tried to resist; she called for help. She saw blood when they cut her, so she could not keep looking when they sewed her up.

She and her sister had had to stay in their beds for seven days. When they tried to comfort each other the women of the house shouted, "If you talk or cry, we will take you to the doctor again. And we'll tell your father you were bad girls." They were in the grandmother's house on the father's side so they suppressed their sobs.

Her father had been in Cairo; the women always did the circumcisions when the father was away. He didn't want to be around for those "female things." The father expected them to be done the Pharaonic way but then he told the mother and the grandmother, "do as you women decide"— as if they didn't do what he wanted.

After the horror of her own experience Fatima had wanted to keep it from happening to her two younger sisters. She told her mother that when they circumcise her two young sisters, it should be Sunna, not Pharaonic. Like her cousin Reem.

Fatima kept saying, "Don't do this to my sisters."

The mother repeated, "Don't tell your sisters. You have to keep out of this. Don't come and tell me this story. We will do this."

It had made no difference what Fatima said. She could not change a tradition even if it was cruel.

Their parents hadn't loved them.

Fatima wiped her nose again and looked out her window. The outside stone wall had a light blue gate to the left of Fatima's window. Next to it were some evergreen trees and further to the right the naked branches of a small not yet fully grown jacaranda tree created a web against the monochrome wall. Staring at the moving shadows, Fatima sat down by her window. Resting her head in her hands, Fatima's thoughts flew up over her enclosure; they floated on through the sandy streets till they pushed open the light green gate to her grandmother's garden by the Nile. They settled in the banyan tree stretching its roots toward the ground, grabbing for a safe footing.

Reluctantly, her thoughts clambered back to her little locked-up garden. In a lethargic mood, Fatima continued to watch light and shade dance on the wall behind the trees, vaguely longing for something to happen. It felt so lonely after Ghada had left.

Suddenly, on top of the wall, a mother cat appeared with two tiny kittens in her mouth. She was moving from left to right. The baby kittens dangled in their mother's jaw by the skin of their neck. Soon after more kittens, who looked several weeks old, were carried in the same manner to the right.

Fatima perked up; she had always wanted a cat but had not been allowed to have one. She kept watching the mother cat going back and forth with her dangling kittens. She was now up to six, Fatima had counted. Six kittens like the six sisters, Fatima was thinking when one little black kitten fell into the leafless branches of the jacaranda bush. The mother cat continued as if nothing had happened. The cat didn't care.

Fatima jumped up to undo the hook high up on her screen door and open it. Hands reaching up on the door unleashed the memory. She saw herself standing like that, hands raised, clutching the bloody knife. The crumbled body of her father next to her on the floor, the pool of blood, widening.

There she had stood, a marble statue. She hadn't been able to move. She had heard the rustle of her mother's dress in the corridor just prior to her piercing shriek. Her mother remained standing on the other side of the fallen man, wailing loudly. She didn't touch the body. She kept screaming as she finally turned away and the crying had receded into their living room.

More figures and faces had appeared behind the prostrate father. Rawia had screamed, in a slightly lighter tone than the mother, and had disappeared to make room for little Jalaa. The skinny girl had quickly taken in the scene before she resolutely had stepped over the father's body and reached up to take the knife out of Fatima's clenched hand. Jalaa had had to pry open Fatima's bloody fingers to get the knife wiggled out.

Jalaa had dropped it with a clank in one sink, turned the faucet full blast in the other and forced Fatima's hands under the water.

Now the kitchen and corridor had filled with screaming, yelling sisters. Zena had been the first one to touch the crumbled man. She had taken his pulse and shaken her head.

"You, Ghada and Jalaa, run over and fetch Uncle Muhammad. But don't tell anything to anybody else. Just get him over here," she had ordered.

"I'm staying with Fatima," Jalaa had replied.

Zena had looked at her and turned toward the living room and yelled, "Rawia stop your screaming and go with Ghada."

Zena had then picked up the crying Selma and gone to the living room to quiet down the mother. "We don't want the neighbors involved," Zena had said to whoever could hear her.

Jalaa had managed to clean Fatima's hands and she had now helped pull her arms down and embraced her. The nine-year-old girl had held her sister tight in the kitchen, where in the sudden stillness the only sound came from the buzzing fly against the window pane. The contorted body of the father had been abandoned on the tile floor.

Gates had slammed, doors had opened, voices had sounded and Uncle Muhammad rushed in. He had looked at Fatima and Jalaa in silence. Quickly he bent over his brother-in-law, took his pulse and bent down to listen for his breath. Then he had quietly closed the eyes of the dead man and called Zena and Rawia to help him carry their father to his bed.

Jalaa's thin body had kept Fatima upright till their uncle had reappeared and said, "Come."

Fatima had put one foot in front of the other, still supported by Jalaa. The uncle had taken Fatima's other arm once they were through the narrow corridor and the two had led Fatima through the white gate, down the road toward their uncle's house.

They had passed some neighbors in the street and ex-changed an "*As-Salam-Alaikum*" and "Wa-Alaikum-Salaam. Greetings of peace to you and to you greetings of peace" in almost normal voices. Some inquisitive glances had elicited a mumble from her uncle, "She fell ill, Fatima."

Fatima had been sleepwalking. The street where she knew each tree, each gate, each stone had looked so strangely familiar. Everything had been too real. The gate to her uncle's house, the rusted color, a little bleached by the hot sun, the scratches in the left side.

Jalaa and Uncle Muhammad had led Fatima through the main house to the cottage in the back. There the uncle's housekeeper Ilham had opened the door and followed them into the small guest house.

They had helped her onto the angareeb and she remem-bered no more. She had fallen into deep darkness. When she had finally woken up, it was night outside and Ilham had been sitting there.

The sun had reached the bushy jacaranda tree with the black kitten on the ground.

Fatima took her hands down from the screen door and held it open with her body weight. She listened to hear if anybody was near. She could distinguish the clattering of pots in the kitchen. That meant that Ilham was occupied. In a flash Fatima rushed out of the screen door and took the few steps over to the jacaranda. She gently scooped up the kitten and hurried back into her room.

Fatima could feel a throbbing behind the soft fur and became aware of her own pounding heart. She sat with the kitten in her cradling hands. She dipped a piece of cotton cloth in her carafe of water and squeezed a few drops into the mouth of the cat. The cat seemed to drink and gratefully Fatima cuddled her baby. She thought of her uncle's words that they would succeed. Hugging her kitten Fatima felt a ray of hope.

Someone knocked on her door.

Quickly she put the cat deep under her bed. Fortunately, it was her uncle and he always entered slowly.

"You look flushed." He looked at the screen door. "Why is it wide open? Did anybody come?"

Fatima stammered, "Nothing—I mean nobody. It was so hot." It wasn't particularly hot. Fatima's uncle looked at her with that look of his. As if he could read her like an open book.

"I just wanted to see if you were okay. I'm sure you enjoyed seeing Ghada. Now I have asked for your friend Reem to come. I will let you know when she can visit." "Thanks uncle, you're so kind," Fatima said. She wanted to talk more with her uncle; but then she remembered she had just put the kitten under her bed. She gave her uncle a hurried hug.

four

It was the New Year but 1999 felt no different to Fatima. Her nightmare men terrorized her in the dark, and during the day her sad thoughts took over. Why couldn't her family have been nice and normal like Reem's? She didn't believe her father when he had claimed that all families were the same. He would repeat, "They are all the same, all families, all fathers." Other fathers were strict too—but not as mean as her father. And did other families have an Uncle Hamid, too?

Fatima's period was about to start. She had her first cramps and as always thought that it wouldn't be so bad if she hadn't been circumcised the Pharaonic way even if she knew her cramps were not caused by her circumcision. But they reminded her of it; she hated her circumcision. It made her feel damaged, patched up. She wanted to be whole.

She remembered how she had often complained to her mother. Her mother didn't answer; she pretended not to hear Fatima's grievances. Fatima went over to her wicker shelves and pulled out a cracker from a bag. She crumbled it in a little saucer and added water. "Come, kitty, kitty." The kitten began to eat.

Now Fatima thought about how she was not supposed to fast because of her period. She would rather not break her fasting as it would only be more difficult to start again;

she then had to make up for the lost days after her period was over. Why was everything made harder just because you happened to be female? She was not supposed to touch the Koran during her period—she was not even supposed to pray while bleeding. She didn't understand why. She needed the consolation of praying. Fatima picked up her kitten and it settled contentedly in her lap. She couldn't accept this notion of "unclean." Her period was her normal body functions as a female. This was part of being able to have children. To give birth to babies—even boys came into the world this way.

She wrote in her diary, *Maybe the Prophet Muhammad doesn't understand these things because he is a man.*

Even if it was only the very beginning of January it was unusually hot. The air was stifling and towards afternoon Fatima felt she could not breathe. Then around the middle of the afternoon, it became eerily quiet and the day darkened. Fatima could scarcely distinguish the sunny section of the wall from the shady one.

The birds stopped singing.

As it became quiet, the sky turned grayish. The atmosphere started to buzz and whistle and the horizon changed to beige. Soon the air was howling and the sky was now a chocolate brown. Fatima realized that an unseasonable sand storm, *haboob*, was on its way and went to her windows and opened them to close the shutters before she tightened the window latch.

A moment later the windows and shutters sprang open, revealing the branches on the trees by the wall flattened towards the house. Ilham ran into Fatima's room without knocking first to help close her windows. They couldn't press them together against the howling wind, and the room filled with sandy air. They lowered their scarves over their heads and Ilham pulled Fatima towards the inside door when she almost stepped on the kitten. Without a word she picked it up and pulled Fatima out into the corridor, where they managed to close and bolt the door.

Ilham led Fatima down the corridor to the kitchen and they sat down on the bench. This was the first time Fatima had been outside of her own room and her small washroom. Ilham passed the kitten to Fatima, who put it in her lap, and they sat listening to the roaring outside. Ilham put a kettle of water on the stove. She was going to soak the *fūl*, fava beans. This kitchen also served the uncle's big house; he preferred to have the cooking done outside of his private domain. It would have been nice with a cup of tea while waiting out the storm if it weren't for Ramadan, Fatima thought wistfully. Her mouth felt dry and sandy inside but she didn't want to drink tea if Ilham couldn't.

The sounds of the howling winds continued for a long time till suddenly the high pitch of the raging sand grains lowered. Then they heard the first splatter of raindrops on the concrete outside followed by the roaring downpour and drumming on their water storage containers.

Fatima turned toward Ilham. "You knew about my kitten?"

"Of course, I did."

"Why didn't you say anything?"

"None of my business."

"But you didn't wonder how I got it?"

"I figured it came from outside—from that orange cat."

"But what about my uncle?"

"He also knows."

"He doesn't mind?"

"We talked about it. We agreed."

"You agreed?"

"Yes, no harm."

"You talked together about my cat?" Fatima leaned against the kitchen wall and was quiet. "What do you think about my uncle?" she asked.

"This is none of your business, but he is a good man."

"But you like him?"

"Everybody likes your uncle."

"Ilham, you're not answering me," Fatima put her arm around the woman.

"There is nothing to answer." Ilham gently pulled Fatima's arm down. "I think the rain is stopping."

The drumming was finally dying down and Fatima knew she had to return to her room. She lingered in the kitchen but Ilham resolutely pulled her arm and they walked through the dark corridor, past Ilham's bedroom, to Fatima's room, where they opened wide the door and windows. The stuffy room instantly filled with fresh air. Everything was covered with a thick layer of dust, and when Ilham went to fetch a broom and dusting cloth, Fatima noticed her perfectly curved foot prints in the brownish sand—small waxing and waning moons.

Toward evening, Fatima's uncle dropped by to see how she was after the haboob. Fatima told him how she and Ilham had struggled with the wind and sand. "I know," her uncle answered with a smile. "Ilham just told me."

"Uncle Muhammad."

"Yes."

"I wanted to ask you a question. I hope you don't mind." Fatima looked down.

"Ask away."

"Well, you seem, seem to get on so well with Ilham, talking and all."

She hesitated then she burst out, "Why don't you marry her?"

Her uncle laughed. "So you are trying to make a match."

"Well, yes."

"What makes you think Ilham is interested?"

"She seems to like you." Fatima stopped herself; she had been close to say more than she really knew—an old bad habit of hers.

"Thanks for the suggestion. I'll think about it. But I came to tell you that your cousin, Reem, will visit the day after tomorrow."

Fatima could barely hide her joy: something to look forward to. But the feeling of happiness only brought the reality of her situation back to her. How could she possibly feel happy about anything?

"Uncle, what do you think they will do to me?"

"We're trying to settle the matter with 'blood money'."

Her uncle petted the kitten. "That's one of the reasons I

am going to Sennar to see our family there. Your uncles owe me a substantial sum of money—and they have it. I'm trying to raise as much as I can."

"Thank you, uncle. But my paternal uncles—would they not consider that my father was very bad to us? They knew about it. They even tried to interfere sometimes."

"You know that's not really relevant. To them a crime has been committed. They will seek justice. And they will not like the fact that a daughter rose in rebellion against her father. That does not go down well in our society."

Her uncle walked to the screen door, his back to Fatima. "A daughter rising against her father—that's a bad precedent in a Muslim country."

Fatima went over to her uncle and took his hand. "But how would they kill me?" she whispered.

"I don't want to talk about this," her uncle said.

"Please," Fatima said almost inaudibly.

"Mostly Stoning."

Fatima suppressed her reaction. Instead she swallowed, hard.

"But these were women nobody could help," said her uncle. "You have a family who will settle for you. You have your grandmother. And me." Her uncle squeezed her hand.

"I know," Fatima breathed and kissed her uncle lightly on his puffy cheek.

Her uncle turned to leave but then he stopped. He looked wistfully at Fatima. Then he asked her if she wouldn't let her mother come and visit her. Didn't she feel like seeing her mother? Without hesitation Fatima answered, "No."

Disappointed, her uncle looked toward the window. Fatima tried to soften her refusal by stroking her uncle's arm. "I just want my grandmother," she whispered.

As her uncle closed the door gently behind him, an image of her mother lying on her chaise longue appeared on the surface of the closed door. The chaise longue was a wedding gift made by a local craftsman, and nobody else was allowed to use it. The mother would loll in her dark upholstered chaise, Fatima herself dutifully dusting the shelves.

She saw it: their living room where the furniture loomed ghostlike against the grayish light through the synthetic fiber of the closed curtains. The solid buffet, the ornately carved cupboard, the heavyset corduroy couch and upholstered chairs crowding the dim room like buffaloes at a water hole. Large framed battle scenes covered the walls: Bedouins with spears raised charged on their foaming horses; a bleeding deer lay felled by the hunter. A female hand had tried to soften the male setting with colorful antimacassars, crocheted doilies, and a bowl of red and white plastic carnations.

Fatima's mother looked equally displaced prostrate in her chaise longue from where she stared towards a crack in the curtains which revealed a street pole outside. One idle hand was hanging over the side of the chair barely touching a transistor radio, which had been turned off.

The mother ignored the girls, who continued dusting and keeping their voices low. A street vendor called out his wares outside. The heavy woman would turn over. "Fatima, Fatima. Hurry. Go get some onions from that old man."

The memory was so real that Fatima felt she was back in her old living room. Relieved, she looked around her present room. She liked it better here. If only IT hadn't happened.

Fatima looked for her kitten and made a purring sound to make her pet come to her. Who was her mother? Fatima had never really thought about that. Maybe her mother had changed and could not remember what it was like to be young. Fatima tried to think of her mother her own age. She was probably very different from now, maybe not cheerful, but at least with some wishes—some secret hope.

Fatima knew that her mother had two older brothers in Sennar, whom they didn't often see. Her mother was the middle of three sisters, and not as pretty or clever in school as the other two. Her older sister, Selma, was both beautiful and smart. Amani had been the normal, average girl, who did what she was supposed to do: went to school and helped in the house afterwards. Eman was the youngest girl and Uncle Muhammad the youngest of them all.

But her uncle had once told her that her mother was musical. One time at a wedding, he had seen her pick up a harp when she thought nobody was watching her. She had plucked the strings and sung with a sweet, quiet voice. It had made a deep impression on him. But he was just the little brother occupied with his own world, and he had never said anything to anybody about it.

When her uncle had told her this, Fatima remembered having often seen her mother sitting with her head by the transistor, listening to music.

Fatima thought about her mother's life. Surely she had helped her mother with household chores—that was required of all daughters. But she did go to school for some years, which was pretty good for her time. Then, as it was for everybody else, her marriage was arranged. Like so many others, she also must have believed that now her life would change for the better. Maybe she had imagined that she would have a wonderful husband and her own house—her own life. Maybe she hoped she would play an instrument.

But the husband was nothing special. And then he imposed all the restrictions she'd believed she'd left behind.

Fatima pondered about her parents' marriage. Then she wondered about their sex life. It was awkward to think about that. Her mother was, of course, circumcised the Pharaonic way; she probably didn't enjoy sex very much. Fatima knew that it was possible to experience sexual pleasure even if you were circumcised the Pharaonic way, but most women didn't. They would just pretend excitement so their husbands could enjoy themselves. Having a son after the first girl was born must have become paramount for Fatima's mother. And then it was a girl, again and again. It must have been a nightmare, Fatima suddenly realized.

And then her mother had those two miscarriages after the first four girls. Fatima didn't know why—the mother never would talk about it. Fatima just knew a little from her grandmother. But maybe they had been boys; they would always think they were boys. It was a curse. And then her father took that other wife. Many would find that reasonable under the circumstances—men took second wives for lesser reasons—some for no reason at all. But that was when Fatima's mother grew ill and seemed to sink into a depression.

Her mother had given up. Her mother was not the only one to despair.

Maybe Fatima should abandon hope.

She cuddled her kitten and rocked her gently. She whispered her name, Orange, and smiled sadly. She had called the black cat Orange because of the tiny orange spots on her cheeks. Tomorrow, Reem would come.

Maybe she should let her mother visit too?

five

Fatima awoke with a special feeling. Even if she had been thinking about her mother most of the night, she knew today would be different. Reem's visits had always been precious to Fatima. She and her sisters had had each other—especially Ghada and Jalaa—but apart from school they were kept separate from the world. Reem had been the messenger from the outside world.

Sometimes Fatima had sneaked in a call to Reem if her parents were asleep or out and had forgotten to lock up the house phone. Sometimes the parents discovered; a lot of shouting and yelling would follow. We'll kill you if you do it again.

The daughters were not allowed to bring friends home from school, but if an aunt and cousin came by the mother had to let them in. Be all polite and pretend she was kind and happy.

Sometimes Reem's mother, Auntie Selma, came with Reem. Then Reem and Fatima would go up to Fatima's room or in the back of their garden and talk about everything. And her mother would call, "Fatima, go to the kitchen and make some tea and bring the biscuits on the silver tray." At least Reem could go with Fatima to the kitchen. Sometimes Reem came alone, but because she was family, Fatima's parents could not throw her out, even if they were annoyed.

Only a cousin could be her friend. Only family. Otherwise it would have been too difficult.

But this visit would not be like the ones they had before. All their hopes, all their talks were from before IT happened. So innocent they had been with all their chitchat about boyfriends. What could they talk about now? What could she hope now?

Fatima sat down to write in her diary but soon dropped her pen and sank down in her memories of Reem. They always cheered her up.

She used to talk with Reem about anything—well, not about Uncle Hamid—but anything from homework to boyfriends and finally: weddings. They didn't have boyfriends. They had some cousins and Fatima had definitely had a crush on Basil. He was so handsome. He had always been gallant—the Sudanese man at his best. But then he had married Amel. There had also been the brothers of some of her school friends. Mainly she would catch a glimpse of one of them, enough to build a whole dream of romance. One glimpse of a handsome boy—that was enough.

But weddings. They could be imagined whether you had a boyfriend or not. Weddings they knew about. The best wedding ever was that of Uncle Arif's son Abdul. Fatima remembered it like it was yesterday even if it was two years ago—the most fun day of her life. It was a big traditional wedding—just like they were supposed to be. Even though there had been trouble and the wedding was almost called off. The bride, whose name was Haga, came from a progressive family; her father was a medical doctor and didn't believe in circumcision. The bride was not circumcised, and had confided it to her fiancé. He was happy about it but told her not to tell anybody else, as it could cause trouble. But the bride's mother thought they were obligated to tell the family of the groom. So the bride's family made this committee of women, who went to visit the groom's family.

The groom's mother, Awatif, was outraged, and some of the women of the family wanted to call off the wedding. But they did a lot of talking back and forth and the committee brought gifts, and in the end they agreed to go ahead even though some of them were still angry.

In spite of that the wedding was conducted in the traditional way and it was a great success. The families gathered in a big house and garden in Omdurman, the home of the bride. Haga wore a western-type white gown with a long veil. The ceremony itself was very short, but then came the days of feasting, eating and dancing.

The third night was the Sudanese traditional "pigeon dance." Fatima relived the evening in the big room full of women all ages from old grandmas who could hardly walk, to tiny girls running around in their fineries. There were some men but mostly women. This was a woman's celebration. The men entered a little later.

The women were sitting or walking around talking, eating sweets, and drinking the refreshing cool karkade. Everyone was waiting for the bride but nobody was in a hurry. Like time didn't exist—that's one thing Fatima loved about those parties.

Then Haga appeared, covered with a shawl. Abdul came from the other side and met her in the middle of the room. They stood facing each other before Abdul slowly removed the shawl. Fatima clearly remembered how Reem squeezed her hand in excitement. Haga covered her face with her hands and Abdul lowered them gently. She was beautiful, with henna ornaments and silver threads woven into her shoulder-length tresses.

Hesitantly, Haga began the "pigeon dance" by tucking in her chin and thrusting out her breasts. Simultaneously she arched her back and stuck out her buttocks, alternately raising each leg from the hip. Fatima and Reem thought it looked funny but the difficulty of the dance and the concentration it took kept them from laughing. With stiff knees, Haga moved slowly and rhythmically backwards. Her arms were kept straight away from her body and she rotated them outwards.

There was a band playing the drums and flutes and a lute. The women were ululating and clicking their fingers. The bride completed the dance perfectly to the end, when she swooned into the arms of her groom.

Fatima remembered the penetrating smell of incense and the fragrance of sandalwood as the bride passed closely by her.

And then came the best part for Fatima.

She walked over to her angareeb and sat down with her arms folded over her bent legs, remembering what happened next.

There were now many more men in the room: a whole group of men in front of the growing band. Most were dressed in traditional flowing white or ebony jellabiyas with *taqiyahs* on their heads. They moved backward and forward toward the musicians with one hand in the air over their heads clicking their fingers to the rhythm. One dancer would break out from the others to do a special performance.

Now onlookers joined the dance and finally some young women were invited to participate. Reem, of course, pulled Fatima out of her seat, and as they were up front, it was easy to join.

Their long cloth wrappings, *tobes*, were off their head but slung right up to their neck, hands extended backwards and breasts forwards. Fatima felt a little shy in the beginning but soon she became absorbed in the smooth motions, intoxicated by the music and fragrances. She moved forward slowly, inch by inch. She sensed Reem next to her. The men across from them lifted their right hands and snapped their fingers over their faces as they bent backwards. Fatima was lost in the dance and the emotions it stirred. It was not meant for any particular man—although Fatima did remember who was across from her.

There was ululating and clapping.

That was then. Fatima stretched out on her angareeb. She glided her hand down over her breast, her abdomen and placed it gently on her crotch. What would intercourse be like? It felt very pleasurable with her hand like that. She pressed it inward. She felt a longing. She could feel something—she didn't know what. Reluctantly she removed her hand. She had almost forgotten about her cramps.

Imagine having a boyfriend. Now she might never get married.

There was a knock on her door. Fatima recognized her uncle's quick rapping followed by a long silence. She just had time to jump up from her angareeb before the door opened and Reem rushed in, followed by her uncle.

Fatima felt disoriented. In the quiet solitude of her room any visit seemed so unexpected—and almost too real. Reem kept hugging her while Fatima tried to get used to Reem's presence. She already anticipated her loneliness when Reem had to leave.

Her uncle gave his usual "hum" and told the girls he would come back from his house to fetch Reem in about an hour.

Reem pulled down her scarf, revealing her long kinky mane—much like Fatima's. In fact, the two cousins looked alike and had often been taken for sisters—even twins. Now it felt good to hug her, her dear Reem. Her best friend with the big smile. She always smiled more than I did, Fatima caught herself thinking. But now Reem's face turned serious.

"I have heard everything from your sisters, especially Ghada. Is it true that you tried to kill your father?"

"I did…but I didn't. I can't even remember anymore. The whole thing is in a blur. I can't remember the very moment. I just wanted my father away."

"There comes a point when we can't put up with it any more," Reem said.

Fatima looked at Reem. Then she said hesitantly, "I guess you're right. It came to that point."

There was a long silence. Reem put her arms round Fatima. Fatima thought she would cry now, but somehow she didn't: Reem could often put words to what she, Fatima, felt.

"Our grandma will come and she will settle everything," Reem whispered and stroked Fatima's head gently. "And we'll all help. We'll fight back. I have talked with my mother. And Basil." Reem broke into that endearing optimistic smile. Basil was Reem's oldest brother. He was a medical doctor who had practiced for two years in America. Fatima had looked up to Basil, and he had always shown an interest in her. And Fatima adored Basil's young wife, Amel, who was a teacher at her women's college. Amel was everything Fatima thought a woman could be: feminine and beautiful, but also smart and educated.

Maybe they would hatch a plan. Aunt Selma always helped with everything.

Reem had already cheered her up. Now she moved right on. "Don't you want to hear some news? About Afraa and the others from school?"

Fatima smiled, "Yes, yes, but after I tell you my secret, which is not a secret anymore," and she bent under her anga-reeb and pulled out the shoe box holding Orange. Reem gently picked up the little kitten. The two girls leaned over the cat and played with it. Fatima showed Reem how she fed the cat and Reem began to tell about Afraa's latest escapade. (Afraa was lucky, she came from a nice and modern family.) She had been meeting her boyfriend, Anwar, secretly in her garden after dark. She had crawled out the open living room window while her parents were watching TV in the back room. They were very passionate, Afraa and Anwar, Reem grimaced, and while kissing in the dark they had fallen onto a prickly cactus and Afraa had screamed out in pain and the dog had begun to bark and the father had gone into the living room and turned on the light. Fortunately, Afraa had closed the window and the father didn't notice that the hook was off. So he went out of the room again while the young couple crouched in the garden.

Afraa had gotten back in unnoticed and up to her room, where she was innocently studying, when her father checked on her. But she had bloody pricks and scratches on her upper arm, and had to quickly invent all kinds of stories about her outdoor gym class to satisfy her father. She was good at that. And thank God he couldn't see her swollen, pricked buttocks.

The two friends were laughing about the story and forgot all about where they were till the uncle's characteristic knock. The girls turned two innocent faces towards the uncle as he entered. He looked at them. Maybe he wondered what kind of mischief they had been up to but he smiled and seemed content that Fatima had gotten a little color in her face.

Reem and Fatima dropped their heads. Now they felt stupid wasting so much time on silly stories but on the other hand it had felt so good to laugh together. And Reem had succeeded in making Fatima forget.

Reem slowly put her scarf back on. She embraced Fatima and gave her an extra hug of unspoken encouragement. Then she turned towards Fatima's uncle, "I can visit Fatima again, can't I?"

"Sure," the uncle said and put his arm around her as he gently led her out of the room.

Fatima tightened her arms around her chest, bracing herself for the loneliness that would descend when her best girlfriend left.

six

Fatima's cramps had suddenly come back, so she asked for two aspirins when Ilham brought her suhoor, the morning meal, before the next sunrise. Her thick hair tightened in a bun, the stout maid came back with the pills. In spite of her stern countenance, she rarely denied Fatima anything.

Fatima thought how she was better cared for here in her prison than she was ever in her home. Life was strange. Here she was a prisoner because she had committed a terrible crime and yet, now she caught herself feeling quite comfortable in between her bouts of anxiety. She liked being left alone. Nobody to order her around. No rushing up early in the morning and sharing the bathroom and being yelled at.

She liked having a room to herself. She liked the feeling of the warm tiles under her feet as she paced up and down.

But, of course, this was but a short respite.

It was the fourth of January and the full moon was fading in the daylight. Fatima had dreamed about her grandmother sitting with her walking stick near the banyan tree, a big bright moon shining behind her. But even if the vision of her grandmother was soothing to Fatima, she was also intensely aware that half the month was gone. Ramadan was half over and the decision would be made soon.

Better think of her grandmother's garden. There it was: velveteen nights with a breeze rattling the long palm leaves with playful intervals; food piled high on the straw mats on the lawn; laughing faces in the moonlight. Stories and jokes rising up towards the sparkling stars.

Fatima's grandmother used to tell stories from "the good olden days" as she called them. "Olden days" were when her grandmother was a young student at the Gordon College. With a radiant face and sparkling eyes she would tell about her youth in the fifties, the time before Independence. The opposition to the British, the meetings, the mobilizing, the camaraderie, the feeling of responsibility. But most of all the hope for Independence—to come into being as a nation. It was as if everybody would be reborn with the birth of their nation. Who could wish that more than the women?

Fatima liked to think back of those happy, optimistic days in Sudan. She liked to think of her grandmother as young. She had been a stunning beauty and so bright in school that her father and brothers supported her entry into the Gordon College, the name of the University of Khartoum before 1956. One uncle gave the family a lot of trouble about this because he wanted Sara, as her grandmother was called, in marriage for one of his sons. The college was co-ed, a radical new idea not accepted by traditional Sudanese. And, of course, the uncle was proven right: Sara fell in love with a history student. She was studying Arabic and the two dated—something you were not even allowed to do today. But those times were radical, in many respects more advanced than now. That was something Fatima's grandmother always complained about: times had changed for the worse with all this religion and Sharia laws. But the uncle had had to find a more traditional bride for his honorable son.

Fatima saw her so clearly, her grandmother surrounded by her adoring grandchildren, wagging her finger saying, not "communist-communist" but "Sudanese communist." She and her friends "supported" the communist party. They had believed in freedom from colonial powers, a more just society, and equality between the sexes.

Sara's father (Fatima's great grandfather) had been a prominent liberal in the Sudanese society. His shady garden had been a social gathering place for the like-minded in Khartoum. Drinking tea and talking politics, the proud father had showed off his literate daughters as they read aloud from the daily newspaper. Think to have a home like that. Her life could have been completely different—and then IT wouldn't have happened.

Fatima walked over to her screen door and stretched. It was the time of the day when the wall was darkened by the shade from the house. Every day she watched the changing light on the wall across from her little window. In the morning the right side lit up about 10 am. Then it turned shady as the sun stood behind the main house and late afternoon it lightened the other side and turned a soft rosy color. That's when she felt most melancholy.

There was Ilham's quick knock on the door. She came in with a little leftover tabouleh and bread and a dewey glass of orange juice. Fatima hadn't said anything but of course Ilham knew she had her period. She also provided the sanitary napkins. Fatima blushed at the thought that she had no secrets from Ilham. Did Ilham know all the thoughts that went through Fatima's head?

Slowly she ate her tabouleh and drank her juice. But now was the shady time when she would lie down on her anga-reeb to wait out the hottest time of the day. What else could she do but daydream or remember things from her life? She stared at the ceiling with an empty head until the splotches and patches of discoloring and peeling paint turned into her grandmother's beloved garden with the big, old banyan tree and the whirling waters of the Nile. The Nile was exciting and luring but also scary and threatening. Now one of the splotches looked like a ram, the ram from when her grand-mother took her along to a village south of Khartoum to the *zar*—a ceremony for exorcising the evil spirits of pos-sessed women. Sudanese women used to have a proclivity for becoming possessed.

Hazy memories of smoke and incense-filled rooms; the women on the mattresses along the walls; the loud frenzied sound of the priestess, called the *sheikha*, and her assistants drumming. A couple of women, heads completely covered by their tobes, moved in contorted dancing on the mat in the middle till they finally collapsed between the seated women.

One possessed woman dressed in a man's clothing was smoking a big cigar. The women were in a trance and any-thing could happen in that mystical atmosphere. It was the forbidden, the *haram*. It was frightening and exhilarating.

The climax came with the sacrifice of the ram, the mem-ory that Fatima always tried to suppress. The ram was led into the crowded room by a servant; he was bleating pite-ously and resisting being pulled in by the rope tied around his neck. The sheikha had the women light some candles and make a circle round the ram while chanting. The women then wound the fine material of the *emma* around the animal, covering it almost completely while continuing the monotonous chanting and circling of the ram, which finally stood still, hypnotized by the drumming, the incense, and the wrapping.

By now it would have grown dark and the moon lit up the scene. The drumming had ceased and the servant pulled the ram outside in the yard, close to where Fatima was standing.

He finished sharpening his knife on a stone while the sheikha took off the emma and placed a bowl under the throat of the ram. The moon glinted in the sharp blade when the servant cut its throat. The ram made a noiseless jerk.

In no time he skinned the ram while the sheikha brought the blood-filled bowl into the room next to the incense jars. Money was collected and dropped into the blood. One of the possessed women was now marked with the blood from the ram on her cheeks, hands, and feet. This was supposed to expel the zar or the jinn from the obsessed woman. But Fatima always thought of the ram as the hapless victim.

The splotched ceiling reemerged from far away while the muezzin called for the sunset prayer.

It had been a hot day for the season but the temperature suddenly dropped and Fatima was freezing. She sat shivering under her one shawl when Ilham finally appeared with her food. It had been a long, lonely day and Fatima tried to engage Ilham in some conversation. But the housekeeper seemed in a particularly taciturn mood that evening so Fatima resigned to her isolation and lay down on her angereeb. Ilham's aspirins didn't seem to work. Fatima drank a little water and wished she could boil it for some tea.

Fatima tried to relax out of her shivers but they seemed to intensify. She also had a headache. Maybe she was ill? She needed somebody's help but she didn't dare disturb Ilham, who was having her well-deserved rest in the room next to her. She would have to endure her discomfort and loneliness.

She suddenly remembered the day she was grounded because she had come home on a bus later than her sister the previous day. She had been made to do hard housework from the early morning, scrubbing floors, washing clothes, and then kitchen work. Chopping vegetables. Chopping, chopping, for hours. Okra, onion, tomatoes, eggplant.

It came back to her. It had been a burning hot day and she had had a headache like now. Then the electricity had gone. The rotating fan in the kitchen had slowed to a standstill as she had begun to cut up the raw chicken for barbecuing. The knife in her greasy hands, sweat running down her face and under her arms, she went into the adjoining room of her mother and asked for an aspirin. Of course, the mother would not give her any. It was not necessary.

"Don't just stand here with that bloody knife," her mother had said. "Get back to work."

Fatima had returned to the kitchen, where the air was so hot that you could cut it into pieces. She wiped her forehead with the back of her free hand. With her greasy hand she filled a glass with tepid water.

She was slicing and pulling the sinewy chicken when her father's voice shot through from the living room. "Fatima, water. With ice."

She would finish that leg before she washed her hands. She scraped and wiggled the bones.

"Fatima, hurry with that water."

She was almost finished when her father's angry puffy face appeared in the doorway. He grabbed and pinched her upper left arm. Hard.

"Didn't you hear me?"

Her arm burned under her father's grip. She was suddenly taken over by the most excruciating rage. The piercing pain in her arm did not let up. Her rage grew and grew.

"Go away," she screamed, and stabbed in the direction of the blurry, ugly monster. "Go away." She wanted to banish that pain, forever. It turned dark around her and she heard ringing in her ears as she stabbed and stabbed. "Go away. Go away." She stabbed the hated voice, the fat blob of meat—all her unhappiness.

She did it. She had done it. Then it had gone quiet. The voice had disappeared. All she had heard was a fly buzzing against the window pane.

She had become aware of her wet raised arm clutching the bloody kitchen knife. She had frozen. She couldn't move and she felt heavier and heavier: pulled down, down toward the ground which felt like hot ice.

The life she'd led didn't exist any more.

seven

It had not been a good night. She had not been able to sleep after she had relived the killing of her father. She had been obsessed like the women in the zar. The whole long night she had tried to suppress the terrible event but then it had forced itself upon her. Now she felt powerless. Only Allah could help. She tried to think of Allah, the Ever Knowing, Ever Forgiving. Ever Merciful. She believed he was.

But the father's family. Would her father's family listen to Allah?

Would Uncle Hamid be merciful?

It was close to dawn and Ilham knocked on her door. Today she brought freshly squeezed orange juice. Fatima felt pleased she had resisted disturbing Ilham's sleep last night and gulped down the refreshing drink. Fatima then dug into a bowl of equally reviving tabouleh but before she had finished Ilham came back with two knitting needles and some purple and blue cotton yarn.

"Here, you need to knit yourself another shawl for the cool nights."

"Ilham. You always think of me."

"*Asma'ai*, listen, it was not easy to find that yarn—but I found it in the *souq*, the marketplace, yesterday."

"And my favorite colors. Did you know?"

"It will give you something to do."

"But Ilham, how could you go all the way to the souq? Aren't you supposed to watch over me?"

"I need to get out of the house now and then. Your uncle was home and told me to go. I needed some other things too."

"Oh, of course, you may need something for yourself?"

"Shall I show you how to?"

"It's okay, I know how."

"Well, I have better get going."

"I know. But...yes, why don't you help me?"

"Look."

"You know, my mother never would teach me something like that. And she wouldn't get us the yarn."

Fatima felt like talking. She could not resist asking Ilham a question. "There is something I have wanted to ask you about—something I believe has to do with female circumcision. Now, don't get angry but I would really like to hear what you think. Do you think women should be circumcised?"

Ilham looked away, clearly uncomfortable.

"Asma'ai, yes, of course."

"You really mean it? But why?"

"You must do it for a 'decent woman.'"

"But what do you mean 'decent'?"

"It is 'proper.'"

"But what about the suffering and discomfort?"

"Women have to take that."

"What about the trouble of giving birth and the re-infibulations?"

"You need to be sewed tight for the man."

"But sometimes the baby cannot get out and… and all the problems. Are you really for that?"

Ilham sat quietly. Then she said hesitantly, "Sunna. Sunna is better."

"Ah, Ilham, I knew, I knew," Fatima put an arm around Ilham again.

Sitting knitting after Ilham had hurriedly left the room, Fatima felt almost happy. Life could still feel good: she loved to knit—knit and think.

Fatima missed a small knitting loop and had to concentrate to dig it up with her pin when there was an unfamiliar knock on her door. Knitting pins in her hands, she rose. Her heart raced.

It was Auntie Selma with her finger raised to her mouth in a hush motion.

"Your uncle doesn't know I came, but I couldn't stay away any longer. How are you, my dear?" She embraced Fatima. "My dear child." She hugged Fatima again and again.

"What a mess. What a mess, my dear. Are you okay?"

Fatima's eyes filled. She couldn't handle so much emotion. Her auntie was always like that—so ebullient. "My dear child."

"Why doesn't uncle know?"

"He didn't want me to come. I have tried and tried to convince him."

"But why?"

"He's afraid of angering Uncle Mohammad, who doesn't want me to see you. He thinks I mean trouble."

Fatima looked in amazement at her aunt.

"And right he is," her aunt added defiantly.

Fatima didn't know what to say.

"You know your uncle is very cautious and he didn't want to antagonize Uncle Muhammad now that he is trying to settle. So here I am," her aunt smiled impishly. I knew my brother was in Omdurman in the souq this morning so I finally got a ride here."

Aunt Selma went over to the carafe of water and poured herself a small glass. "Ramadan or not Ramadan. An old woman needs a little water."

She drank a few sips and pronounced, "We have to get you out of here." She sat down lightly on the only chair.

"Nothing else will do. I'm talking with my son Basil and we're hatching a plan."

"Does Reem know?" Fatima asked.

"She knows we're talking and she's going to be our messenger with you."

Fatima sat down heavily on her angareeb. She sat in silence while her aunt was sipping water. Aunt Selma had been the model, successful Sudanese wife. She'd given birth to ten children of whom five were boys. She had been the female head of a large and thriving household, respected and admired by her husband and entire family. The husband left the running of the household to his wife and asked her advice about everything concerning the children.

Although the marriage had been arranged and she was married before she was sixteen, it had gone well and the husband and wife had come to love each other. Their aunt's one complaint was that she had missed becoming a tennis star. She had lived near a club with tennis courts and used to watch as a young girl. But her parents did not think in "terms of tennis" and she never got the chance to even try. As she would exclaim with a rueful smile, "I am a frustrated tennis star."

She had had one large sorrow, when her youngest, Muhammad, drowned in the Nile. He had been a daredevil attracted to the water and had refused to listen to his parent's cautions. "Everybody has their own sorrow," her auntie would say.

"But how are you, auntie?"

"Well, well, quite well. I have my little continence problem." Fatima's aunt had always been open-mouthed. Fatima blushed a little.

"You know from my Pharaonic."

Fatima knew the story about Selma's botched Pharaonic circumcision. Her mother had been out of town when some zealot aunts and grandmothers had taken matters in their own hands. The same thing happened with Fatima's own mother but it was only in Selma's case the circumcision had gone very wrong. The youngest of the three sisters Aunt Eman was only Sunni—Fatima's grandmother didn't let up her guard this time. But for Selma the mutilation had made intercourse almost impossible. Her father had sent her to Sudanese doctors and finally a specialist in London.

"It's a barbaric tradition and the Koran doesn't even require it." Aunt Selma knew her Koran in order to be able to quote it in her not infrequent arguments. Otherwise, she was a strong proponent for keeping religion a private affair and disdained the Sudanese government for using religion to suppress people.

"But why do women still support it?" Fatima said. "Like my mother."

"It's because they feel vulnerable and they want to be accepted. They think they will be respected if they are ardent in this matter. The only way we can change it is to promote the milder Sunna version. When everybody then sees that it isn't the end of the world and doesn't cause promiscuous living, then the attitudes will soften. But it takes time. As you know already the British outlawed it. That, of course, called for patriotic resistance." Once Fatima's aunt got started on the subject there was no stopping her.

"Auntie, I have something to tell you—something I have never told anybody." Aunt Selma's flow of words stopped abruptly.

"It's about Uncle Hamid."

"What's about Uncle Hamid? Your uncle mentioned that you seemed to bring up Uncle Hamid repeatedly?"

"Yes, but I couldn't tell my uncle. I felt too ashamed." Her aunt looked questioning at Fatima who hesitated. Then she said very quickly, "Uncle Hamid touched me in my private parts."

"What!" her aunt exclaimed.

Fatima looked down.

"When?" her aunt shouted.

"When I was a little girl."

"Well, exactly when?"

"As far back as I can remember. But the last time was in second grade; then I learned to avoid him."

"Dear, oh, dear. That too." Her aunt started to take big gulps of water. "Why didn't you tell me or your grandmother before?"

"I told you, I felt so ashamed. I somehow felt I was at fault."

"What shall we do now? This won't help us. Your uncles, the males will stick together. They won't admit it. They will say you're lying. Why didn't you tell before? How come, you suddenly tell now that you're in trouble?" Her aunt had finished her water and went to pour another half glass. "We can't prove it. We have no evidence and he was not caught in the act. Why didn't you call for help?"

"I tried, but I always lost my voice."

"This is bad." Her aunt was going to take another sip but then refrained herself. "How much did he do?"

"Well, he stroked with his hand on my private parts under my panties." Fatima hesitated, "And then he tried to stick his finger in a little and it hurt."

"Oh, God, maybe it even protected you that you were circumcised so tightly so he couldn't." The aunt got up and started to pace the floor in agitation.

"He also did something with his other hand under his jellabiya. Now I remember."

"Stop, I don't want to hear any more. Well, I do. Was there more?"

"No, that's it. That's how I could escape when he took his left hand off me. Now it comes to me. Then he couldn't catch me," Fatima said.

Her aunt was pacing. Then she abruptly stopped. "I know. I will talk with Suad."

"Aunt Suad? But she's not, not friendly."

"No, that's true. But she may listen. She's already on a warpath with her husband. This will be a strong card on her hand if she threatens to bring this out."

"But how could this help me?"

"I will tell Suad to influence Uncle Hamid for a settlement."

"But why should she?"

"You may not understand, but this is about power: her husband wants one thing so she settles on another. Sudanese women operate like that. She will force him to make a concession to her."

Fatima didn't quite understand but one thing for sure, Selma knew how to operate. She usually got things her way.

"But I thought you just said I should leave the country?"

"Yes, that's one plan. But we need both plan A and plan B." Aunt Selma broke into her roguish smile. Settlement is better than leaving forever."

"Forever..." Fatima's voice faded.

Her aunt rushed over to her. "I need to be out of here before your uncle returns." Hurriedly, she hugged Fatima several times. "We'll find a way and soon your grandmother will be back. I will keep you informed through Reem."

Another intense hug. "Bye, bye, my dear. My dearest."

eight

Fatima felt grateful as she lay down to sleep that night. Aunt Selma always made her feel upbeat; even if her arguments could be confusing, Aunt Selma could get things moving. She made Fatima believe it was possible to do something. That you didn't have to sit passively with your hands in your lap. People loved Selma—or hated her. Fatima wasn't surprised Muhammad disliked and distrusted her.

Suddenly the thought of leaving Sudan had crashed like a wave of sorrow over Fatima. Forever, Aunt Selma had said. Maybe Fatima would never see her sisters again. And Reem. Never again would she sit under a tree and talk with Reem. And look over the Nile. If they could make a settlement; there was no place in the world she would rather be than in Sudan.

But the next morning Fatima felt optimistic and still energized by Aunt Selma's visit. Strange, but she felt at ease in her room, in her body. She got up and went out to her little wash room in the corridor. She looked at her hazy image in the broken mirror. She wrinkled her nose critically; it was a little too big, she thought. And her skin was too dark. Her eyes could be bigger but her mouth was full and nicely shaped. She rather liked her mouth with the two half moons of the upper lip. That was her best feature. And her hair, which was very thick and kinky. She pushed it up with a hand; it really drove her crazy to wash and comb it, but she liked it. She liked dark hair better than blonde. Blonde looked like a doll's hair.

That's what she thought: she was not beautiful, but she was real.

But why had they named her Fatima? She disliked that name—so old-fashioned and sad. The prophet's favorite daughter was Fatima. Still, she would rather have been Jamila or Suzanne? Something more cheerful—and modern. Especially Suzanne. That sounded like a woman. And sensuous. Fatima put cold water in her face and dabbed it lightly. Then she returned slowly to her room.

She lingered indecisively until her little kitten began to play with the tassel on her sandals. Absentmindedly she picked up the cat and cuddled it against her chest. Fatima's glance settled on the small jacaranda tree outside her window. A few buds were swelling on the bare branches and one had opened up in a cluster of luscious lavender-blue flowers. They were blooming early this year, Fatima thought. Maybe it was the heat from the wall?

Not a breeze. The night had been cold again but it was already warming up. Right now the temperature was perfect—caressing. Her room was entering that quiet stillness, which was both soothing and sad at the same time. It was the middle of the day when her wall was in the shadow of the house but the sun was burning down on the roof.

She could do a little knitting. No, she did not feel like knitting. She put her cat gently into her little shoe box and stretched out on her angareeb. She thought of her grandmother's garden and her banyan tree where she was lying on the grass in the shade of it...with a boyfriend next to her. Anwar. No, Basil. No, not Basil—somebody looking somewhat like Basil.

Slowly she glided her hand down over her breast and stomach. Again and again. Gently she put it between her legs and pressed a little. It felt good. She needed to do it more. It came again this big longing. She did it again a little more vigorously—the pressing. Deep down—it must be in her vagina—she felt those contractions. An underground tunnel of squeezing and expanding. Her banyan cave by the Nile, the dancing, gyrating women at the zar; a tugging pull sucked her into the subterranean whirlpool till suddenly she felt a great knot come apart in the center, spreading to all sides in tingling currents. The waves spread and spread till they finally calmed into little, lazy flaps on the shore.

She was not sure what had happened. She kept her hand tightly against her lap, amazed. That must be it: she had reached a sexual climax all by herself.

Imagine there were such delights in herself—in her own body. Fatima looked around her room. It looked the same, yet it felt so different, as if there were a whole hidden world behind the ordinary façade of the familiar furniture and walls, beneath the hot floor tiles.

Fatima lingered on her angareeb. She felt weightless—floating just inches above the mattress. She remained motionless and almost stopped breathing for fear of disturbing that airy feeling. Vaguely she realized there was something in life she had not been aware of. Why hadn't she discovered this before?

Surely, it was because she had never had a room to herself.

Then it occurred to her that her parents had something to do with it: they had kept her away from learning that life could be different.

She sat up with a jerk. What if she had not been circumcised? What if they had not removed her clitoris? That's why they did it. She sensed it—like the first sun rays after a cold night—that she could have known more about pleasure. She could have known more about herself.

She got up and sat down on her chair. A feeling of regret turned into beginning anger. Her old anger which she couldn't explain. It was just there like a deep shadow right next to her—the bottomless dark water wells she was afraid of falling into as a child.

Then another thought occurred: Was this sinful?

What she had experienced must be what they called a sin—a haram.

What would the Koran say?

Reluctantly she reached for the Koran even though her period wasn't quite over.

She leafed around till she found the Treatment of Women section. Mohammad talked about "indecency." Fatima felt confused; "indecency" was such a wide concept. But deep down she felt that her act probably would be referred to as an "indecency." Even if her sexual behavior was solitary and wouldn't harm anybody, she guessed that all sexual acts should be between a married couple to be judged "decent." The path was a narrow one between the many pitfalls.

Of course Fatima had talked with her girlfriends about sex and pleasure and desire. But not about girls doing it alone.

She had heard talk about boys masturbating and it was condemned. But like everything with boys it would be rejected in public while in private, those boys would be considered virile. Fatima never had heard about girls masturbating; she hadn't thought it could happen to a girl. She hadn't known that girls maybe weren't so different from boys.

She slumped in wonder in her chair. Then she straightened up. She felt empowered: she could learn things on her own and she could be different from her parents. They had kept her away from the world; it would be up to her to make her own life.

Only now it was probably too late. So strange she only began to feel like a person after she had killed her father. It had been like she couldn't think or feel for herself as long as she lived in his intimidating shadow. He had been the authority; unfortunately, somebody else would take his place. That was the Sudanese society.

She felt like talking to somebody about her thoughts, her new-found feelings. She only had Ilham near by but all this was completely outside of Ilham's world. She could talk with her uncle but even though she could exchange ideas with him, he always argued in favor of the social norm. Still, she would try to talk more with him.

Then there was her grandmother. She would agree that Fatima could have her desires and be a believing Muslim. But she was from "olden days;" Fatima would need somebody more contemporary. Aunt Selma wasn't afraid of being controversial but all her daring and rebelliousness seemed too hodgepodge to Fatima. Aunt Selma had the right spirit but ultimately, she was confused, Fatima decided. Her own sisters were too ignorant. That left her Reem. Maybe she could talk with Reem, but although she trusted her, it was like Fatima's crime had put her in a different place, irreversibly.

Maybe she couldn't talk to anybody.

Nobody else could feel like she did right now. On the one hand she felt a growing power and a sense of freedom; on the other side she had a gnawing feeling of uncertainty. She was a believer and wanted to do the right thing. Was it wrong to be wanting pleasure? Maybe it was immoral to masturbate and maybe this was somehow connected to the killing of her father? Maybe once you started to sin one way, you would do it another way, also?

But she didn't really think so. Yes, she wanted pleasure but not at the expense of others. And she was filled with love for so many people and for Allah most of all. Her father had been an evil person, Fatima felt sure of that. He ruined the lives of her and her sisters. Should she just have accepted her unhappy fate?

Fatima's thoughts would go round and round; thoughts were so powerful. She had to rein in her reflections; her best way to do that was to return to her grandmother's garden. So back to it. Back to the banyan tree.

But that was where she had just been.

There was the familiar knocking sound. Gratefully, Fatima looked toward the door as her uncle entered.

"How is my 'rosebud'?" Her uncle hadn't used this pet name since she killed her father. He patted her cheek gently. Fatima noticed his tired eyes in spite of his smile.

"I have talked with your paternal uncle Muhammad about settling the matter with some large payments. May I?" Her uncle pointed to her desk chair and sat down heavily as Fatima nodded. A deep flush rose in her cheeks as she thought of her recent activity.

"He didn't say outright no, but he didn't make any commitment, either. He wants to wait to discuss the matter with his two younger brothers when they are all together. And he doesn't want to make it easy for us."

Her uncle wiped his forehead with his handkerchief. "I don't know if it is because they are particularly greedy or vengeful. I cannot believe that they would find justice in having a young woman...."

Fatima didn't linger on her uncle's words—or his omission. She was trying to adjust to his presence. She thought of what she had just been doing. "Maybe my grandmother could help with the payments," Fatima said from far away.

"She would certainly want to. But she doesn't have that much money. They will want a lot."

"Maybe I should try to escape?" Fatima asked, as casually as she could.

"I have thought of that, too," her uncle answered matter-of-factly, to Fatima's surprise.

"The problem with that is that then the case will remain unsettled and can develop into a protracted family feud."

"All the trouble I have caused." Fatima's eyes welled up.

"You didn't mean to. Of course, it would have been helpful if you weren't so hot-headed. Not that you have it from strangers." Her uncle tried a faint smile.

"But your father drove you crazy," he added with a sad look. "I don't hold you responsible. If only I could have averted it," he added ruefully.

A cloud of dust rose up over the outside wall as a big lorry passed by.

"Why did we girls have to be circumcised?" Fatima suddenly asked.

"That's a funny question considering our present circumstances. Why do you ask that now?"

Fatima flushed deeply. "I guess I sit here so much alone— with time to think of so many things."

"Yes, that is not good. But to answer your question, I tried to convince your parents to do the Sunna."

Fatima got up and tried to hide her flushing. Her uncle pretended not to notice.

"And when your grandmother on your father's side heard of this she made sure to have the circumcisions done secretly, before anyone could stop it."

"Each time?"

"Each time. It's impossible to keep an eye on you all the time. If somebody insists on doing something, they will eventually have their chance. At least I had managed to convince the women to have you anesthetized locally."

"But why? What I wanted to ask was why it must be done? Why do we have this tradition?" Fatima ignored her blushing.

"You are persistent," her uncle smiled a little. "And I guess you want an honest answer."

Fatima nodded, "Yes, I trust you uncle, even if you're…."

"A man. I know, I know. So forget about all the silly things people say, and forget the superstitions. It has been done to curb the sexuality of women, to make them less interested in sex. With other men that is," he added.

"But that would make them less interested in sex with their husband?"

"It could. But often it is worse than that. They still have the desire—because sex is also a mental thing—but then they sometimes don't have the capacity, and many have problems."

"How do you know?"

"There she is, the smart aleck." He smiled. "People talk, and I know personally from my dear wife. Rawia had many problems—and she was even only Sunna."

"I am sorry uncle; it was just something I was thinking about."

"It's all right. You have a right to ask. We can talk more about it another day. I have to go see Amani now."

"How is my mother?" It felt strange to say "mother."

"She seems to be doing a little better. For a while she refused to eat and she couldn't sleep. She seems a little calmer now. And she asked me how you were doing."

"If you want, my mother. She can come and visit me."

"You mean it?" Her uncle's face lit up. "Then I'll bring her over tomorrow."

"But remember, I was going to see Reem, too," Fatima quickly added.

"Sure, that's a deal: first your mother, and then Reem." The uncle gave Fatima a bear hug.

"And one more thing," Fatima said. "Do you think it at all possible that I could have a little fan? I would put it on only when it is the very hottest."

"Yes, your room tends to get very hot." Her uncle was reminded to wipe his forehead. "I will see what I can do." He headed for the door.

"And uncle, one last thing."

"Yes," her uncle stopped.

"Any news about Ilham? I mean, have you talked to her?"

Her uncle walked back toward Fatima. "I'm afraid I don't have good news."

"What did Ilham say?"

"Well, she didn't say anything. She sort of turned away, and she didn't accept."

"Typical Ilham. Maybe she's just shy. And she never talks."

"She mumbled something about it was good how it was— as things were right now."

"But uncle, don't give up. You have to give her time."

"And you are the expert?"

"Well, no, but I have a feeling. I know Ilham. Maybe I could speak to her."

"I don't think this is any of your business."

"I know, uncle, but you realize she is extremely reserved. And proud," Fatima added quickly.

She put her arms around her uncle's shoulders.

nine

The next day, January the seventh, Fatima awoke feeling anxious about her mother's visit. She wondered if she had a special reason to come; or something to tell Fatima. She also tried to prepare herself by thinking about her mother and her childhood. Fatima had come to understand that her grandmother probably hadn't been a good mother. She had been ambitious and children didn't interest her. She had had lots of domestic help in order to cultivate her literary and political interests.

Fatima's mother, Amani, had gotten very little attention. The least pretty and least clever middle girl, she had been shown her place in the family hierarchy. Compliantly, she had fitted into her assigned roles. Fatima was trying to comprehend why her mother had always seemed so passive to her. Now Fatima promised herself, she would make an effort to listen to her mother. Really hear what she had to say. She wrote in her diary, *I will talk with my mother for the first time.*

Fatima had barely put down her pen before Ilham knocked on her door. Her knock was very different from her uncle's. Quick and light—but she didn't wait before she opened the door like her uncle did. Ilham said her mother would come in about an hour's time and her uncle would pick her up when the visit was over.

As Ilham turned to leave, Fatima stopped her. "Ilham, can I ask you something?"

Ilham didn't answer but slowed her steps without turning.

"Ilham, I know you don't want to talk much but, but it's about my uncle."

Ilham turned.

"He seems very unhappy."

"Why?" Ilham burst out. But then she looked like she knew what Fatima was getting at, and said no more.

"Don't you think you could be happy with my uncle? He is a good man."

"It's good how it is."

"But it could be even better."

"How?" Ilham already seemed to regret speaking at all.

"If you were husband and wife."

"It's good how it is."

"Don't you want more out of life?"

"I'm at peace. Al'ham de l'Allah. Thanks to Allah."

"Is that all you want, to clean and cook and be a domestic help?"

"God provides."

"You could have your hands freed for some of the interests you have. I have noticed how you're always trying to get to your knitting, your bead necklaces and flowers." Behind her enthusiasm, Fatima was beginning to doubt what she was saying. She tried a new angle, "I think you're just afraid of your own feelings."

Ilham looked as if she was going to say something but thought better of it.

"Afraid, because you do love my uncle."

Ilham turned and walked towards the inner door. She opened the door, turned half around and said, "*Mumken.* Maybe".

After Ilham left the room Fatima wondered why she was so keen on making this match. She truly believed it could make her uncle happy but maybe Ilham was too much of a domestic to feel comfortable. Fatima had an increased nagging feeling that she simply had turned a busybody for the lack of a life of her own. But now she would have to concentrate on her mother's visit.

A moment later Ilham showed her mother in. For some reason Ilham seemed a little embarrassed.

Her mother had aged since Fatima last saw her. And she had put on weight—she probably still spent most of her time in that chaise. Her mother was wrapped in a white tobe, reminding Fatima that she was in mourning. Fatima got up and walked toward her mother, who gave her a quick, light embrace with her face averted. She went on to the only chair in the room and sat down heavily while Fatima settled on her angareeb.

The mother slowly lowered the tobe from her head and loosened it around her shoulders. She looked around the room and said nothing. Then she pulled a handkerchief from her sleeve and dabbed her face. It was already warming up.

Mother and daughter looked at each other.

"Your sisters send you greetings."

"Thank you. How are they?"

"Al'ham de l'Allah. Thanks to Allah."

Silence.

"Jalaa sends you this." The mother pulled out a flat parcel from her loose sleeve.

"How is Jalaa?"

"Al'ham de l'Allah. She is well."

"How is her school?"

"The teacher says she is doing very well. Al'ham de l'Allah."

Silence descended again and Fatima began to open the little present. Her hands trembled a bit. It turned out to be an old post card so weathered that Fatima could scarcely see the picture. Finally, she could see that it was a photo of a banyan tree with the faint contours of the Nile in the background.

"What is that?" said her mother.

"It's a banyan tree," Fatima's eyes welled up. "Like the one in grandmother's garden."

Her mother said nothing. Fatima could see that she had no interest in a banyan tree or in how much it meant to her daughter.

Fatima turned the postcard in her hands. Even if her mother said nothing she had received solace through Jalaa's gift.

She tried again. "How are you doing, mother?"

The mother looked sad and sighed. "Al'ham de l'Allah." She looked at some undefined spot on the wall and the oppressive silence clamped down. The mother pulled out her kerchief again and dabbed her face. "It is very hot."

"No, I don't think it is so hot. It was cold last night," Fatima said curtly.

But suddenly Fatima felt it was warm and a prickly heat was getting to her: a thousand needles were stinging her all over, injecting a nervous energy with each prick. She got up from her angareeb and began to pace the floor. She tried to keep her movements calm so as not to agitate her mother.

There must be something she could say. Something to make her mother respond. But everything she thought of would only make her angry.

"Mother, is it true you used to love music?"

The mother looked at her as if she was coming from far away. "Who told you that?"

"Uncle Muhammad."

"That was long ago. It's not important now."

Fatima watched her mother dab her temple with her crinkled kerchief.

"Did you ever play an instrument, mother?"

"It's of no consequence."

"Well, what is important?" Fatima increased her pacing.

Mother and daughter looked at each other.

"If you will not say anything, I can tell you," Fatima said. "It's important you are my mother and you are visiting your daughter and I killed my father. You could say something to me. You could try to help me—like you never did." Fatima's voice was no longer subdued. "Did you come here just to say nothing?"

The mother had gotten up from the chair. "I don't know what is wrong with you," she said. "You were always so ungrateful, so...so...selfish. As if you were different. And look at what you have done." The mother leaned forward and broke into hysterical crying as her uncle quickly entered the room.

"Amani, Amani. Calm down. Calm down," he said, leading the mother out of the room. He looked over his shoulders and nodded to Fatima that he would return. Fatima had a glimpse of Ilham as she closed the door behind her mother.

Trembling, Fatima sat down at her desk. She tried to calm her shaking and picked up her pen to write. But she was too agitated and got up to pace the floor. She was still walking barefooted up and down the warm tiles when her uncle returned. He sat down on her chair with a sigh.

"Well, that didn't work out."

"Why were you and Ilham there right away when my mother started yelling?" Fatima wondered aloud.

"We were in the kitchen talking, and I couldn't avoid hearing your raised voices.

"I don't know why my mother even came to see me."

"Well, I suggested it. I knew she was worried about you and I thought it would do her good."

"She didn't want to see me."

"I thought it might be good for you, too."

"Uncle, what you don't understand is that my mother doesn't love me. Nobody understands—nobody knows."

Fatima stood still in the middle of her room. "Why were my parents like that?"

Her uncle was silent, then said in an unconvincing tone, "They did their best. They tried to shape you and your sisters into obedient daughters."

"They told me I was nothing."

"They tried to bring you up according to tradition but they sensed rebellion in you. Like the time you didn't return home."

"I should never have gone back," Fatima exclaimed vehemently.

"No, you did the right thing."

"And always you, and everybody, told us to be patient. 'Traditions cannot be changed overnight.'" Fatima imitated the monotone admonition of a parent. She was pacing again.

"That is true, but things are changing if you look closely. More women get education. Wives have more freedom than before. They used to not leave their marital home except for with legs first. There is more flexibility. More women work."

"Maybe that is so. But what about me? My parents wouldn't allow me to bike when I was eight or something. 'It isn't proper for a woman,'" Fatima sneered. "So maybe my daughter may bike—but that doesn't help me. I wanted to bike—what am I waiting for? Think of Aunt Selma and her pathetic wish to play tennis. All she could ever do in her lifetime was send sad looks to those tennis courts where the men and *ferenjis* were playing—and having fun."

"Calm down, Fatima. Calm down. You have your points, but you're born in the culture you're born in. At least your father allowed you to get an education—and that in spite of having six daughters."

"That wasn't my father. My grandmother arranged it when he was out of the country—and she paid."

"You sound very angry now."

"I am angry. I'm...furious."

"So, so...We're just discussing these issues."

"But they are not just issues, they are real things."

"True. But to get back to your father, he accepted your being educated nevertheless. That was a big step for him. You have to see it in context."

"I know. But that doesn't mean young women have to put up with everything. As you say yourself, things are going backwards in this country. Women have to cover up more. People are lashed for drinking alcohol even if they are not Muslim—like the Southerners. The north is trying to force Sharia upon the south. We cannot accept it. We must fight it." Fatima was close to yelling.

Her uncle looked at her but said nothing.

Fatima went over to her open door and looked out through the net of the screen. A bird was singing outside. The tones were rising and descending harmoniously. Uncle and niece listened in silence.

"The world is so beautiful. Why do we always make it so sad?" Fatima said through the door.

"Tomorrow I will bring Reem, as promised." Uncle Muhammad turned in the doorway. "And a small fan."

After her uncle had left the room Fatima went back to the screen door to look out. In the silence she could hear the voices of all her visitors in the room. Her uncle's deep, worried baritone; Reem's cheerful chatter and giggles; Aunt Selma's indignant outbursts; her mother's slow, monotonous voice. It was like they were all there, talking, even after they had left.

She sat down to write but she was still too agitated. She would take a bath first. She opened the door to the house and entered the darkish corridor, where she searched for the handle to the little toilet room on the right hand side. She could smell Ilham's cooking at the end of the corridor. There was a squatting toilet and a tiny sink with a faucet on the wall. Fatima retrieved the orange bucket leaning up the wall under the sink and began to fill it with water. She preferred to wash midday, when the water was warm. She took the little soap and her wash rags and carried them into the room.

She took off her blouse and bra and soaped her body. Then she wiped herself off with gentle strokes. She plopped the rag in the tub and reached for her towel and rubbed her upper part thoroughly. She dropped her towel and held her breasts in both hands. She closed her eyes and enjoyed the feel of the firm weight in her hands. She breathed deeply before she interrupted herself and covered up to get the next tub of water for her lower part. She would need two tubs to clean up after her menstruation.

She concentrated on her task of wiping her smooth body. No lingering now but holding the warm washcloth on her private parts all her good intentions melted away and she stopped to feel the wet, warmth of the cloth in her crotch. After her secret pleasure the previous day it would be very difficult not to give herself that new enjoyment she had discovered. Fatima dressed hurriedly.

After she had tidied up she sat down again at her desk and thought about her mother's visit. Something had changed. She felt a strange calmness when thinking about her mother, a detachment—she could no longer harm Fatima. The mother had nothing to say; she just reacted; she was a victim because she didn't try to understand.

It occurred to Fatima that she saw her mother but that her mother would never see her. There was no reason for Fatima to fight with her anymore. She should use her energy elsewhere.

She began to write in her diary, *I see my mother as a victim of Sudanese traditions that demand a woman submit to her role as wife and mother—with no other options for her.* She dropped her pen. If only she could get the chance to do something helpful for Sudanese women. Help educate them, make them think. Make them enjoy their own lives. The women of her own generation—it was too late for her mother's.

But what could she do now?

Fatima could smell the delicious fūl, cooking under Ilham's deft hands. She was ravenously hungry.

Tomorrow Reem was coming and she would tell Fatima about Aunt Selma and Basil's plans. Fatima was ready. She wrote, *After my mother's visit, I know I will have to leave this place. There is no hope for me here.*

ten

Ilham had brought the most delicious fūl the night before. Ilham knew how to cook the beans just right: hard on the outside, mushy inside. Then she mashed some of them to make the sauce nice and thick. On top ripe tomatoes and *girgir*, arugula, cut up with raw onion slices, a generous dab of sesame oil, a sprinkle of lemon and salt and pepper. The combination of the hearty soothing bean with the fresh tomato, girgir and tangy lemon was the most heavenly blend of tastes Fatima knew. Add to that a thick, cool mango juice. Contented, Fatima had fallen asleep and slept like a stone for many hours.

But then a nightmare had awakened her. She had dreamed she was being forced to marry Uncle Hamid. Somehow she knew it was a dream, but it was still awfully scary. Half-awake, she thought she would have to kill herself. If she were forced to marry Uncle Hamid she would rather die.

She had a stomach ache when she stood up—maybe it was all those beans? After fasting, she had a bad habit of eating too much.

But she loved Ilham's food and the atmosphere of Ramadan. She would think of that. The quiet days, the merry nights. The days of empty streets in the scorching sun, the occasional columns of dust whirling round like small dancing dervishes. People lying in the shade of the big banyan trees next to the Nile; the taxi driver, his mouth ajar, sprawled on the back seat of his open-door car; the street vendor prostrate under his cart loaded with bananas.

But not everybody was sleeping. Hidden behind the walls of kitchens and pantries and sculleries, the women, wives and mothers, grandmothers and daughters, were busy preparing for the breaking of the fast, *fatur*. Every day during Ramadan was the same; but the highlight was the Holiday of Eid, which Fatima always spent at her grandmother's. She and all the other women of the family slaughtering chickens, feathers flying as they were picked, hands bloodied taking out the intestines, the cleaned birds piling up like naked corpses ready for their clothing of spices.

As a little girl, Fatima had helped pound cinnamon, cloves, coriander seeds, black pepper corns, fennel, chilies, and dried vegetables like okra and tomatoes into a mellow ochre paste in a small wooden mortar. Led by Aunt Selma, all the women sang and joked, even though they were thirsty and a little weak from hunger.

After dark and prayers, they fed the men. Sitting in big circles around the large plates of food on the porch, the men would dig in with a piece of the fermented pancake-like *kisra* to grab the meat and sauce. They chewed and chewed, glinting sauce dripping down their chin. They wiped it with the backs of their hands and dug in as fast as they could swallow. They burped. The women smiled and emitted contented clucks; the more the men burped the better. The men were satisfied; then the women could relax and eat, too.

Waiting for the women's turn to eat, Fatima would climb her banyan tree. She grabbed the roots and found a curve for her foot as she pulled herself upwards to the branches above the loose roots. There she was on the top of her tree-house and she could survey her extended family, men eating, women serving, and kids running all over. This was her family, and if she got tired of them she could just turn her back and gaze over the luring waters of the river. From the safety of her tree she could dream away, her thoughts like a small boat bobbing the waves, disappearing into the wide, wide world. This was her outpost. Mostly she was there alone— Ghada was too scared to make it up so high—but in recent years Jalaa had climbed up with her and they felt that special bond, separate from the crowd.

Fatima's family had some weathered photos of the banyan tree, taken when a British Colonel lived in the house before the independence. The British took good care of their trees and planted many new ones. The banyan tree was fully grown around a dying sycamore when her grandmother's father had bought the house and garden. Sycamore gone, the main trunk of the banyan tree was big and knotty and hollow in the inside. Fatima felt how the tree stretched back in time; if she listened to the wind in its branches it whispered about the Sudanese history all the way back to Colonial times.

Finally, the women spread out the straw mats on the lawn to feed themselves and their children. Forgetting all about the Sudanese past, the hungry Fatima would rush down from her tree. The mats felt soft on the thick grass of the lawn, which was the pride of the grandmother. In the dry season it yellowed and threatened to dry up and she had her workers and the children around the house carry buckets of water up from the river to sprinkle the grass. In the dry season she kept just small patches of the lawn green and they always sat on that part, listening to the cicadas chirping and swatting after the mosquitoes that flew into their ears with a buzz.

Once she fled the country she would never again be able to celebrate Ramadan in her grandmother's garden.

But all she could do for now was to wait for Reem. It was only eleven o'clock, she could see on her garden wall. Still a long time to wait. Maybe she would lie down on her anga-reeb for a little while.

She must have been deeply asleep when she heard from the end of her banyan tunnel a repeated knocking sound. Closer and closer till she realized that her uncle was knocking on her door and waiting for her to say yes.

Confused, she jumped up. Again she experienced the sense of intrusion as Reem rushed up to her and gave her a long embrace. Reem brought vague but familiar smells of spices and dust from the street; they encircled Fatima like greetings from Khartoum.

Reem turned to see if the door had been closed behind her. Unraveling her long scented scarf, she related the latest news from their friends to Fatima. Afraa had broken up with her boyfriend Anwar. Reem thought it was because she had her eyes on his older brother, who was a lawyer.

"That Afraa, she knows what she wants," Fatima said admiringly. She tried to suppress a sneaking feeling of envy;

she really did want Afraa to have all the boyfriends in the world.

"No more silly-talk today." Reem looked Fatima in her eyes. The two girls stood facing each other. They were the same height and stature. Their kinky hair was similar, although Reem's was quite a bit shorter than Fatima's.

"Listen. Today we have no time for chitchat. Aunt Selma and Basil and I have a plan. We know Uncle Muhammad is trying to get some money from our uncles in Sennar next week, just before the end of Ramadan. I will come and visit you when our uncle is out of town. My brother will bring me."

"That could make Ilham suspicious," Fatima said.

"I have already asked our uncle if we can visit, and he has agreed and will tell Ilham. He also thinks it may do you good to see me at the end of Ramadan, when you may be getting more anxious again. And he trusts Basil. Soon will be Eid and I will have to stay home and help in the house."

"But?"

"No but, just listen." There was no stopping Reem once she got going. "Basil is leaving for Egypt with Amel and they will take you with them. You will fly to Cairo."

"Fly?"

"Yes, fly. In an airplane." Reem lifted her hand and illustrated a line of flight. "Taking you out of the country is the only way to save you. I don't know how much Basil knows about our uncles; he may have heard rumors. But you know how he feels. He really cares for you. Besides, he is modern—he is against all this suppression of women."

"But what will happen to him when he returns to Sudan?"

"That's the whole point, he is not going back. Listen to the end without interrupting." Reem could be very bossy when she got keen.

"He means to immigrate to America. But he will pretend he is just going to Egypt."

"America?"

Fatima's heart started to pound. She had read things about America. She had seen pictures, even some American film. But she had never imagined going there; somehow it didn't appeal to her. Also she didn't appreciate that she wasn't consulted about the plans; like she had no say. It was her life and these could be irreversible decisions. But no time to think about that now.

"Now, don't begin to hesitate. This is your only chance. Maybe your father's family decides to have you killed, or maybe they ground you for life. Remember the story about Aunt Amani, who was locked up in a house till she went crazy."

"But how will I get out from my room? There is also Ilham."

"Basil will divert Ilham while you change clothes with me. I will bring my big canvass bag so you can take some things with you."

Fatima thought about her diary.

"Basil will come back in and pretend he is late and rush you out wrapped in my tobe. He will stand between Ilham and you if she happens to be right there. Basil will turn you away and push you out in a great hurry and you will speed off in the car. If Ilham enters later she may not notice it's me tucked up in the bed and if she finds out, she may not tell anybody till the next day, when your uncle returns. Also it is good timing. It's after your meal and everybody is busy preparing for Eid. They are preoccupied. Nobody suspects anything at this time."

"Poor Ilham. This may get her into trouble."

"She'll have done nothing wrong."

Fatima was trembling. She walked over to her screen door to calm down. She could definitely not imagine being an immigrant in America. Then she looked at Reem with a jolt of horror.

"But what about you? You will get into terrible trouble."

"Uncle Muhammad is in debt to my mother after she lent him a lot of money. She has signed papers. He knows she will demand the money if he gives her trouble, and he cannot pay back. Then he would lose his house; he will not go after me."

In her confusion Fatima felt a ray of hope. Was it that simple? Then it struck Fatima in dismay. "But maybe they would turn my sisters into scapegoats and punish them?"

"They didn't do anything. They can't be held responsible. Maybe some trouble—that's all."

Fatima's eyes welled up, "But…"

"I know what you think. But the answer is that we are happy to do this for you. We women have to help each other."

Reem put her arms round Fatima, who had begun to cry. "Pull yourself together or it will be suspicious. Don't ruin our plan."

Reem shook Fatima and pulled out a pair of scissors.

Fatima stared in horror.

"I have to cut your hair the same length as mine," she said. "It's only a detail but we have to prepare as well as possible. I have to do it now."

Fatima tried to subdue her emotions, while Reem deftly began to cut her hair. It was no small job to cut such thick hair and even though Reem had a lot of practice with her own sisters, they both worried that time was running out. Fatima's thoughts were chaotic while she tried to address the many issues her escape entailed. The implications were stupendous to her, and all the time she had a nagging feeling her life had passed out of her power. She felt a growing urgency to obtain control. But how?

In the meantime, Reem tried to calm her and they kept talking in low voices, refining their plans. Now and then Reem ordered Fatima not to move her head.

Completely absorbed, they didn't hear the gentle knocking of their uncle, who had entered their room before they noticed.

"So this has turned into a ladies' beauty parlor," their uncle laughed.

Fatima looked confused, but the unflappable Reem answered, "I thought I could cheer up Fatima with a little haircut."

"No harm in that," said their uncle.

eleven

The morning after Reem's visit, Fatima was thinking of the pictures she had seen in a Home and Garden magazine in the school library. Homes with swimming pools and Cadillacs driven by clean shaven Gary-Grant-type men. Those were very old magazines, but somehow the images had survived. Fatima didn't know much about America except that it was the land of freedom and human rights, the land of President Kennedy and now Bill Clinton. It was the land where everybody could become a pop singer, "moon walking" in a shiny suit like Michael Jackson. The land of opportunities—that was the great attraction. People could be as different as they wanted, as long as they had talents and worked hard and were idealistic.

America was a great place—the only problem was that it wasn't Sudan. What would she do in America?

I would go to university, Fatima dutifully wrote in her diary, and then dropped her pen. She couldn't really imagine herself in America. Those glossy magazines in her dusty school library—the life they pictured didn't seem real. Fatima would rather live in Sudan. If only she hadn't held that knife in her hand. Maybe she would have hit back at her father with her bare fists.

But done was done and she would have to escape. Yesterday Reem had reminded her of their Aunt Amani, who had been locked up because she did not obey her husband. He simply moved to another house with his other wife. Then Amani could sit there and rot away till she went crazy. Nobody helped her. They said she was not obedient. What had she done? Fatima didn't know. Probably the husband had just gotten tired of her.

But house arrest. Fatima had tried that. Now that whole miserable affair came back to her. How she had been invited to Reem's by her Aunt Selma, and her parents gave in for this one time like they were a normal family. From Reem's house they'd gone to see a mutual friend; Aunt Selma gave them a lot of freedom to go to friends' houses. The girls were having such a good time visiting in the friend's little garden pavilion that Fatima had been tempted into staying for the night. It was of course completely reckless of her, but it was as if everything was possible in that nice atmosphere. It made the bad feeling of her home so unreal and distant. Maybe she could just forget about it—or take a little break from it. But, of course, life was not like that; it had just been her wishful thinking.

When Fatima hadn't returned home that evening, her parents had gone to Reem's house and run around to all the houses because Reem's mother was out, and they didn't know where Reem and Fatima were. Then the other uncles became involved, and another cousin, who knew about the garden pavilion, came running to the girls to warn them that Fatima's father was going crazy. "You have to go back home immediately, or else."

Fatima had become scared. Suddenly it had dawned on her how she had shown bad judgment. Now she really wanted to run away, but she had then decided she had to do the "right thing," which was to return home and take her punishment—for punished she would be. That she knew. But she didn't know how bad it would be; if she had, she wouldn't have returned home.

As soon as the door was closed behind her in her father's house the father had struck her with his shoes—and then with anything he could get hold of. He threw her against the wall. Blood started to run from her temple after she hit the corner of the cupboard. Sometimes her father was like the devil. In the past, Fatima had been afraid he was going to kill her; this time she was sure he would. He said it: "I will kill you. I will kill you."

He had locked her in her room. She couldn't go anywhere. Not to school, not to family and of course not to friends. She was in prison. She was black and blue all over. Her older sister, Rawia, got house arrest, too, even though she hadn't done anything; this was to set an example for her older sister. Rawia and Fatima hadn't been close ever since; their father had destroyed their friendship. Their mother did nothing to help them.

When school started after the May holidays, the two sisters were still not allowed to go. Now the grandparents told her father, enough was enough, but he didn't listen. Everybody tried to talk to him—except for her mother. Both her parents pretended Fatima was not there; she was invisible.

Then her older sister, Zena, who had been visiting a relative in Northern Sudan, came back. She was shocked over their situation and she told her father every day that they had been punished enough and they needed their education.

Zena was the only one who could sometimes talk to their father. He hated her less, Fatima believed. Maybe because when she was a little girl their father still hoped he would have a boy. He'd hated the other girls from the start.

Every day Zena approached her father. Every day he shouted at her. But she didn't give up and Fatima would never forget that.

Finally, Zena came into their room and told them they had to go and talk with their father themselves. Fatima was terrified when at last she went to his room. He made her ask him every day, day after day, till finally he said, "Tomorrow you will go to school, you and your sister. You will go together and you will talk to nobody. You leave and arrive at the same time. If there is free time after your classes, you go to the library. You don't talk to anybody; you have no need of friends."

Fatima's cheeks burned as she remembered how her father had humiliated her. "And don't ever come to tell me that you need anything—or to see anybody," he had continued. "Don't ever ask me for anything." Then had come his final threat. "Just remember, your father is right next to you all the time; he knows everything you say, everything you do—and he can come any time."

But he couldn't come any more. Or could he?

There was a quick light knocking and Ilham stuck her head in. She had a small fan under her arm. Relieved, Fatima got up and went over to Ilham and put her arms around her.

"Ilham, you're like a mother to me. You take such good care of me."

The serious woman gently but resolutely took Fatima's arms down. "Al'ham de l'Allah," she mumbled.

"Sit down, let's talk a little bit. I need to talk a little."

Reluctantly Ilham sat down.

"You know, my mother never would do anything for us girls." Ilham nodded in a way that could be either yes or no. Then she said quietly, "She took care of you."

"She never talked to us except to tell us what we couldn't do, couldn't have."

"She was bringing you up."

"But she never kissed us."

"You can show love other ways."

"Yes, but she didn't." They sat in silence. "But, Ilham, do you think she was a good mother?"

Ilham hesitated. "*Yani.* I mean there are better ones. But you have the one you have Al'ham de l'Allah."

"What I really wanted to talk about…"

"I know, but I have things to do." Ilham got up from the angareeb. "I came to tell you that your uncle will see you tomorrow before he leaves for Sennar. Your Aunt Selma will bring Ghada and Jalaa this afternoon." Ilham passed the fan to Fatima.

"Thank you. Thank you, Ilham."

"Ma' Mushkila. No problem."

The room was turning warm. Fatima went to her door and opened it and re-closed the screen. Not that the air was cooler outside, but the approaching midday shade gave the appearance of coolness. Fatima sat down and read a little in the Koran. Even if she felt she knew it inside-out by now, it didn't answer so many of her questions—questions related to how she should be living her life. She could not help but feel the Koran was written for men—and for men long ago. There should be a Koran for women, she thought and lowered the book. She put it on her small table and went onto the floor to do her midday prayer. She turned towards Mecca and bent her head. She tried to empty her head for the prayer.

Praying did make her feel good. It gave her peace. She would try to stay in that peace till her sisters' visit. She lay down on her angareeb. She turned on her little fan at the end of her bed. She closed her eyes and felt the hot air caressing her body as the little vanes churned merrily. Titillating streams of warm air.

If she were married, this new habit of hers would surely disappear.

Fatima was fast asleep when Aunt Selma brought her two sisters. As usual, she felt disconcerted by the sudden activity in her quiet place.

"Ghada, Jalaa. How are you?" She embraced her two sisters again and again. She thought Jalaa had grown since she saw her last—she looked even skinnier than before.

Then her aunt hugged her several times and said, "Everything will be okay. Have courage." And when the two sisters were bending under the bed for the cat she whispered, "Your sisters know nothing—keep it that way." Loudly she said, "I'll leave you alone. Have a good visit," and she gave Fatima one long intense embrace.

After their aunt had left, the three sisters settled in a circle on the floor and played with Orange, teasing her with a piece of cloth till she tried to catch it with her paws.

"I'm glad you killed father," Jalaa said dragging cloth and cat across the floor.

"You shouldn't say that. Even if he was evil, you mustn't kill a person." Ghada took over the cloth.

"Some people are not people—just scum." Jalaa grabbed the cloth from Ghada.

"Maybe. But nothing has changed for us." Ghada let Jalaa take over with the cat.

The two sisters told about their home where everything was the same, even without their father. Their mother was not sitting in her chair so much, but she directed the girls in their chores as if the father was still there. Maybe their mother wanted to keep up the impression that everything was the same. The father's spirit was still ruling. The mother's new role was to live in his memory.

"But won't mother have to remarry? She can't live alone," Ghada exclaimed.

"Maybe she'll have to marry the horrible Uncle Muhammad as a second wife," Jalaa said sarcastically.

"Then you would get directly under his power, but Aunt Fatia would know how to stop him from taking a second wife," Fatima said. "Their marriage is unhappy enough with just one wife."

"All marriages are unhappy," Ghada declared.

"Maybe not all," Fatima said after an interval. "There's Uncle Muhammad and Rawia. That was a love marriage. Then of course, she had to die," Fatima said.

"There's Aunt Selma. They have a happy marriage," Ghada exclaimed.

But then the sisters agreed she was successful because she chose the role that had already been chosen for her.

"She's just like these proud Sudanese women who all want to paint a beautiful picture of their life," Ghada summed up Selma's marriage story.

"I will never marry—never in my life," Jalaa burst out.

"Why?" Ghada said.

"I will not have daughters whom I will be forced to have mutilated."

"But maybe at that time you can have daughters whom you don't mutilate," Fatima said tentatively. "Maybe that could be your role as a mother, to break the vicious circle." She started to talk about it when Jalaa interrupted her.

"Fatima, we're wasting our time with talk. What are we going to do about you?"

"We never heard back from the sheikh," Ghada said. "Those men, they don't even feel they have to answer us. That's the fact."

"Our grandmother will be back soon and maybe she can make a settlement," said Fatima. Aunt Selma was right; she couldn't tell about the plans to escape. She would love to tell her sisters, but things might go wrong, and she could protect them better if they knew nothing.

"But she doesn't have enough money, I fear," said Ghada.

"So we sisters have all talked about it—well, not Selma, she is too young, and not Rawia, either. We do not know if we can trust her after she was punished with you. But we have talked about how we could sneak you out of here,"

Jalaa said. "You can steal the gate key from Ilham—we know where she keeps it, in her apron pocket. She takes her apron off at night. You unlock the gate and we sneak you out in the night. We would get a taxi and take you to the bus stop."

"But we don't have enough money," said Ghada.

"We have already been stealing from the housekeeping money without mother observing. We buy the food so she doesn't know," Jalaa informed proudly.

"Then you don't eat enough," Fatima exclaimed.

"Oh, we eat plenty," Jalaa said in a convincing tone. "And we lie about the meat prices" she added triumphantly.

"But the bus. To where?"

"We're not sure yet. Probably towards Darfur. Cannot go to the south because of the war. Towards Egypt they may find us easier. We have to elude any pursuit; it will not be easy. But we will do it," Jalaa said in a loud voice as Ilham entered the door.

The three girls closed their mouths in unison but Ilham merely said that Aunt Selma sent greetings. She was outside with her driver to pick up the girls.

For sure Ilham had heard what they had said—they had spoken so loudly. They could only conclude that she was pretending not to have heard.

twelve

Yesterday Fatima had been certain she would leave Sudan. Today she was not so sure. She was touched over her sisters' plans for an escape; although she didn't think it sounded very realistic. But the real problem was that she wanted to be with them—not an ocean away from them.

But she didn't know if she could trust that her uncle and grandmother would succeed in making a settlement. Her uncle kept assuring her. But was that because he really believed it, or was it to calm her down? She couldn't be sure.

Fatima went to her screen door and pulled it towards herself to open her outer door. The air was fresh and crystal clear. Winter morning air: she had loved it when she and Rawia used to rush to get to the minibus for their college. Fatima leaned against the rough door post and thought of the morning cold driving through the dusty streets to Omdurman. Crossing the bridge over the Nile—flickering shade and sun. All the girls hurrying for their classrooms, recognizing faces, hugging Reem, laughing and joking with Afraa. That had been her life.

She sat down on the cold doorstep and rested her head in her hands. Her teacher Mrs. Badri drawing her beautiful Arabic letters into flowing garlands of words. How Fatima enjoyed her classroom, everybody bent over their desk taking notes while the room grew warm and everybody forgot the time, themselves, their homes, and their problems. They were a group of girls together to learn. Together they had new thoughts— ideas that expanded their world wider and wider, far beyond their city on the river.

Education was the key. Fatima returned to her favorite thoughts about education, how once you had an education the next step was to get a job. This was the second step to get out of the house. Then in many cases the family benefited from the woman's salary and the men finally saw the light. Sometimes the family could not make ends meet without the additional income. Slowly, slowly it would get accepted that women had jobs outside of their home. They would then earn respect for contributing to the house keeping. Fatima saw it so clearly. And then you had fewer children and you knew more about the outside world and they no longer treated you like a child. And then you got some women into politics and then, and then, you got female *ulama,* scholars, to study and interpret the Koran and the *hadith,* the tradition. They were all believers, Fatima and her friends, but they didn't think the men interpreted the Koran fairly for the women.

Just quietly, the women did these things and step by step they changed conditions. The men had the power so the women had to be the wiser and the more subtle. The Sharia law was there for the men; the women had to figure out ways around it.

And here she was, sitting. What had she done? She had wanted to become a teacher like Mrs. Badri and now she had ruined everything. She had blamed her father but she herself was to blame. It was her own doing.

Fatima recognized her uncle's knock and rushed up and closed the screen door as silently as she could and just had time to turn towards her uncle as he entered. He had a thick notebook under his arm.

"This is for you. I thought you might run out of paper, you're writing so much. Then you will have plenty while I'm in Sennar."

"Thank you so much, uncle. And thank you for the fan. You always think of me."

"Well, I think I am making a little writer out of you," the uncle said cheerfully.

"If only I can live up to your expectations," Fatima sighed.

They stood in silence; Fatima was a little taller than her uncle. Then her uncle smiled encouragingly. "You want to hear some good news?"

"What do you think?" Fatima almost smiled.

"It's about Ilham."

"She accepted," Fatima exclaimed.

"How did you know?"

"I thought she would. I talked to her."

"Ah, so it's your doing," the uncle chuckled.

"No, of course not. So, what did you say?"

"I told her I would have to find her another position if she did not want to marry me."

Fatima looked incredulously at her uncle. "You did? What did Ilham say?"

"She said, 'Well, I don't think you should find another position.'"

Her uncle looked almost young right this moment, Fatima thought.

"Anyways, we just had a long talk in the kitchen and we agreed that we could live together and feel great affection for each other. You know, after Rawia, it could never be the same. But we feel affection—and respect."

"Mabruk. Congratulations. I'm so happy for you." Fatima kissed her uncle before he turned toward the door.

Then she quickly asked, "Are you and Ilham going to have a wedding celebration?" Now she was talking about weddings while she was planning to escape behind her uncle's back. Her uncle, who was like the loving father she'd never had.

"That depends. We're not having a wedding unless you can celebrate with us."

"Ilham is a good person. You're lucky to get her as a wife."

She would be betraying her uncle.

"Yes, and now they can no longer put pressure on me to marry somebody else."

Fatima remained quiet; all she could think of was that she wouldn't be there for her uncle's marriage.

Her uncle misunderstood her silence. "Yes, it should be you marrying—not me."

"Well uncle, I no longer think of marriage." That was not true either, but Fatima felt ashamed to say anything else.

"I don't believe you," her uncle patted her cheek.

"I have spoiled everything, uncle."

"It is difficult but we will settle, Al'ham de l'Allah. Then we'll see."

"Uncle, I don't regret about my father but I am sorry because it put us all in a bad position."

"I failed. I failed."

Fatima looked questioningly at her uncle.

He got up and walked over towards the screen door. Bent forward, he suddenly looked very old.

"I don't think anybody will miss my father. But uncle, the truth is: I must deal with my anger. And my hot temper."

Fatima's uncle patted her cheek gently. "Allah Karim. Allah Karim. Will you be okay till I'm back in two days?"

Fatima nodded and blushed.

Her uncle looked tenderly at her.

This might be the last time she ever saw her favorite uncle.

As always when her uncle had left her room, Fatima went through their conversation. She pondered every word her uncle had said, his intonations, his silences. She thought of what she had said, what she could have said. She would have liked to tell her uncle that she hoped to marry one day—but that it wasn't important now. She just wished she could do something useful. For women especially. But that was just empty words now she had decided to escape behind her uncle's back.

She was trapped by her own doing and something her uncle had said kept returning to her. Her uncle blaming himself for what she did. The more she thought about it, the more disturbed she felt. He made it sound like she was not responsible for her own actions.

She took out her knitting and began to knit. That was exactly what the Sudanese men had always said about women, that they were not responsible; they were more like children—impulsive. That's how they could justify the laws that took away the rights of women and turned men into their caretakers. That's why a woman could not travel alone, why her witnessing only counted for half of that of a man. That's why a man could divorce his wife by just saying "*Talaq,* I divorce you," three times.

Her uncle had implied the same thing. But he was wrong. She was responsible for her words as well as for her deeds. She could not run away from them. She would not.

About an hour after her uncle had left, Aunt Selma, hardly knocking, popped in her head. Like the last time she placed her index finger over her mouth. "Hush, hush. I know your uncle just went to the mosque to pray before he leaves for Sennar." She put her arms around Fatima, "How are you holding up, my dear?" Without waiting for Fatima's answer, she continued. "All is in place. Basil and Reem will come, and Reem will stay behind while you leave with Basil and Amel."

"Thank you auntie, you're all thinking of me. I don't know if I even deserve it."

"Shush, shush. Deserve or not deserve. Of course, you deserve it."

Fatima hesitated. "But, auntie, what do think would happen if I didn't escape?"

"You must leave, must leave. I'm not in doubt about it. You cannot stay. No way."

"But Uncle Mohammad and my grandmother are making a settlement."

"Anyways, you will not be safe. Maybe Uncle Mohammad makes a settlement but somebody else may go after you.

Even from the next generation. You know how fanatic some of those young men are."

"Maybe you're right."

"You bet I'm right. Why do you want so much to stay in this awful country?"

"It happens to be my country. And my family."

"Some family."

"My sisters. And I would like to do something in Sudan."

"What is it you would like to do?"

"I would like to finish college—and to teach."

"But you could become a teacher in America too."

"But that would not be the same. And I would like to do something about the female genital mutilation."

"That you can do with the immigrants in America. You know, the problem is there too."

"But it wouldn't feel the same."

"Feel the same, feel, feel." Aunt Selma looked like she became aware of her mocking tone; her face turned thoughtful. Then she exclaimed, "Think of this Somali woman, Ali, in Holland. Think how much she is able to do."

"I am not like her. Also I am a believer; she is not. Also, I think she must have an awful life, all the threats. She must feel very lonely." Fatima made a pause, "But I do admire her. Only I am different."

"Maybe you are. But my advice is to avoid the Muslim countries. It's much better in the West."

"That is maybe true—but it's not my culture. I think I would feel very lonely in Europe or America."

"That's nonsense. It just takes some time and you'll feel at home there."

Aunt and niece had been so involved in their discussion that they hadn't heard Ilham, who had entered the room with freshly squeezed orange juice. She looked even more stern than usual; she was clearly not happy about Aunt Selma's presence. She placed the juice on the table and remained standing next to it.

Aunt Selma looked quizzically at the hovering woman. The room turned silent. For a long interval the three women remained motionless. Turned toward Fatima, Ilham finally said, "I have not been informed about any visit today. Your uncle only gave his permission that Reem and Basil may come by tomorrow evening."

Aunt Selma got up from the angereb. "I must be off. I had mentioned to your uncle that I would drop by just now. Bye, bye, my dear. Soon it will be Eid and happier times." She embraced Fatima several times before she left the room, ignoring Ilham.

When Ilham returned with the steaming beans Fatima got up from her chair and asked Ilham to sit down.

"Ilham, stay with me a bit."

"You know I have cooking to do. It's almost Eid."

"But Ilham, I feel lonely."

"Okay then. Just for a little while." Ilham sat down, her back erect on the edge of the angereeb.

Fatima went back to her chair and Orange jumped into her lap. Orange always kept her distance from Ilham.

"Tell me, Ilham. How was it in your family? Tell me something about yourself."

"Yani, I grew up in a village. We were poor; we rented a small plot of land from the big landlord. Our house was mud and straw. There were many rats."

"How many sisters and brothers?"

"That was the problem: thirteen. Well, ten survived. But we were very poor, and that's why my father joined the army to fight in the South."

"Did he hate the non-Muslims?"

"Hate? No, he didn't hate anybody. We needed the money. But then he was killed and they paid us almost nothing." Ilham tightened her shawl.

"I'm sorry, Ilham. But do you have some good memories?"

"I don't know. I helped in the house always, and took care of my little brothers. The house was bad. It was a long way to the river for water."

"What was the worst day in your life?"

"The day my father died. My oldest brother was just 15 and he went to join the army the same day we were told about my father's death."

"I'm so sorry. But surely you had a good day?"

"The best day was when the postman came with the letter from your uncle asking if I could help him in his house. He was the cousin of a cousin of mine, and had heard about me. God is just."

"Imagine the nice house you'll have now with my uncle."

"Alham de l'Allah." Ilham looked much younger when she smiled, Fatima thought.

"How old are you, Ilham?"

"About thirty-two."

"You could still go back to school."

"I don't know." Ilham hesitated. "But I would like to learn to type—and be a secretary." There was a new, keen tone in her voice Fatima had not heard before.

"Of course, you can do that. I'm sure my uncle will support it."

"Yes, he does. We already talked about it. This was important to me, I told him."

Fatima was amazed. "I knew it, Ilham. I knew you would want to do something. But now, first is the wedding."

Ilham made a move to get up and leave.

"Ilham, can I ask you something very personal? I know I shouldn't, but from woman to woman."

Ilham looked at Fatima without answering.

"What about your wedding night?"

Ilham clasped her hands and looked questioningly at Fatima.

"I mean, are you nervous?"

"Your uncle is a good man. Allah Karim."

"Yes, but it may be painful."

"What about that?" Ilham rose and straightened her shawl. "God is just."

Fatima stood up and grabbed Ilham's hands.

"Will I be okay?"

Ilham turned and looked at Fatima.

"Ilham, please, please tell me."

"Ensha'Allah, Allah willing." Gently she pulled her hands out of Fatima's grip. She stepped back to leave but then she moved forward and embraced the younger woman.

thirteen

That night Fatima didn't expect to sleep. She tried not to think of her planned escape, it made her too jittery. She thought about Ilham out in the countryside and her hard life. She saw her patiently carrying water from the muddy river. If she could only be like Ilham, God would provide. But she was not like Ilham, and she had even risen against her father. It was like rebelling against God. How could she expect mercy now? She was a sinner. It was clear in everything she did and thought. Now she planned to deceive Ilham. There was no consolation and she would just have to wait out the long dark night. Resigned, she pulled her blanket over her weary body.

Fatima had finally fallen asleep only to wake up from a nightmare. In the beginning of the dream Fatima heard some noise by her door. But it was still a dream.

"Here she is," a man's voice whispered. She let out half a scream before she was gaggled with some emma material. She was pushed over and her hands tied on her back. A burlap bag was put over her head and she was thrown roughly over the shoulders of another man.

He carried her past Ilham's room. If only she could scream so Ilham could have alerted her uncle. But like sometimes in dreams no sound came out. And maybe this saved Ilham for these men would not have treated her gently. She heard the gate rattle a little; the man carried her down the street, turned a corner, and through another street. Fatima was thrown onto the back seat of a car. A man smelling of cigarettes sat next to her. The car started and they went full speed over the potholed roads.

The men were silent, only the car rattled along. She could hear that it must be an old car. So this is the end, was all she could think. Her initial terror already submerged to a profound sadness. Her life would be wasted. No more. Nobody. " Allah Karem. Allah is merciful," she kept repeating as the car shook her body.

The engine came to an abrupt halt. The door was flung open and the cigarette man pushed her out onto the sandy ground. He gave her a hard jerk in the back to walk. She stumbled; he took off her burlap bag.

There was a streak of dawn in the horizon. The stars were fading. She could see several men in a semicircle in front of her. In front of them was a deep hole. She thought she recognized a son of Uncle Hamid among the men but she didn't have time to think about it for the cigarette man lifted her up and carried her a few steps before he dropped her into the hole. She felt a sharp pain on the temple on her head and then a great nothingness.

She woke up to the sounds of the night. She was trembling all over. She stretched out her arm and touched the surface of her rough wall. It felt familiar. She was in the safety of her own room. Reassured, she just lay still and waited to calm down. She talked to herself. She told herself that her dream was just based on her fear of uncle Hamid.

It was to be expected; it was just a nightmare. And she was leaving, anyways.

Finally, the first rays of sun hit her wall. The light chased her bad dreams away and her nightmare already seemed so unreal. It was too horrible to be real. The night was her fears; the day was her real life. There was some juice on the table from Ilham. She had not heard Ilham come in.

After a while she went over to her door and opened it for some fresh air. She looked through the screen at the jacaranda tree with all the greenery behind it. Two more jacaranda flowers had opened up into a cascade of flittering shades of blue and purple. Soon the green leaves would unfold and the whole tree explode into color and fragrance. But by then her room would be empty.

Orange rubbed against Fatima's ankle. Absentmindedly, she picked her up. Reem had promised to keep Orange and take good care of her. You will be happy with Reem, she whispered into the fur of the kitten. But she would miss her sisters, and a surge of pain rose through her chest. Surely she would find a way to see them later on. She would write a note to each sister; she had lots of paper after her uncle had given her the new notebook.

But first she began to write her grandmother. *Dearest, most beloved grandmother. You were always my role model.*

Fatima dropped her pen. She couldn't continue writing, she couldn't face the thought of not seeing her grandmother again.

Fatima got up and began to pace the floor wondering if she would ever be able to see Sudan again. The tiles were warm and smooth. She would even miss her room. She went back to her desk and wrote Jalaa to study hard and eat enough. Then she could come to her in America. Her tears were smearing her writing now. Fatima went out to her small bathroom to get a bit of toilet tissue to blow her nose.

Throughout the long hot hours of the very last day in her own room, Fatima tried to write at her desk, only to get up and pace till she threw herself exhaustedly onto her anger-eeb. But there was no rest for her this day and even if she told herself that her nightmare was only a dream, it still left her scared. She tried to visualize the grandmother's garden but the images flickered and broke up like a photo torn to pieces. Even her thoughts began to tumble into confusion. She thought of one thing but before she finished the thought it was interrupted by another. She could lose her mind like Aunt Amani.

Fatima pulled herself together. She would have to focus; she would write her uncle, the one who saved her from going crazy with terror right after she killed her father. If it weren't for him, she wouldn't have made it.

11 January 1999   B'ism'illah. In the name of God.

My dearest uncle,

You were always there for me and you saved me after the terrible thing happened. I cannot express to you my agony over fleeing the country before thanking you for everything. My only consolation is that I believe you would agree to the course I have taken.

I will remember every single word you have spoken, all our discussions about traditions and change, marriage and dating, *religion…everything. I know I have been impatient, but worse has been my anger. Now I hope to transform my anger into good work. Maybe if I live in America I can help Sudanese refugees there…maybe…*on and on she went, hoping to convince her uncle that all his encouragement had not been in vain, she would live up to his highest expectations. She ended by wishing him and Ilham happiness together. *Mabruk, Congratulations, my dear uncle. You and Ilham deserve happiness together.*

While she was tearing the page carefully out of her notebook, she thought her uncle would understand.

Writing to Rawia would be much easier. Determined, Fatima opened up a blank page in her notebook:

11 January 1999   B'ism'illah

Dear Rawia,

I know you're angry with me. Please let go of your anger and you will feel much better. I promise you. Don't forget father did this to put enmity between us. Do you want him to succeed?

Remember all our times together and our nights in our grandmother's garden.

We will meet again under better circumstances. En'sha'Allah. Allah willing.

Your loving sister, Fatima.

She tore out her letter to Rawia and folded it carefully before putting Rawia's name on it. The letter writing gave Fatima relief. She leaned back in her chair when it hit her again that she would be leaving her country and her family. But then the final confrontation with her father washed over her. She got up to retrieve her shawl from her pile of clothes by the far wall. In the middle of the floor she broke into a sweat and returned to her writing desk. Moment by moment she relived the terrible encounter with her father. Her despair that hot day, her sense of futility as she stood chopping vegetables. Her feeling of utter hopelessness when her mother turned down her request; her surprise at seeing her father, who never set his foot in the kitchen; her terror as he pinched her arm, her pain, and her fury—her unspeakable rage that knew no fear.

She had been possessed. She now saw it clearly that she had been a victim of her own passion. And her own uncontrollable anger had hurt her more than her father had. He had caused it, yes, but she had let him.

Fatima thought how the zar event had been for the women to be together and help each other get rid of their jinn. Maybe their evil jinn spirit was their frustration. Fatima had failed to get rid of her jinn.

She sat unmoving for a long while. Then she picked up her pen and wrote on top of the last page of her new notebook. *I attacked my father not to kill him, but because I lost myself to my pain, rage, and abandonment. Even so, I am responsible for what I did. So help me Allah.*

Fatima closed her notebook and stared at her bare wall turning rosy in the setting sun. She was still sitting there when Ilham brought her break-the-fast juice an hour later. Soon after, Ilham stepped in with Fatima's evening meal and reminded her that Reem and Basil would arrive shortly. Basil worked late at the hospital so they couldn't come earlier. Also it was important for their plan; this way Ilham should not see "Fatima" till early before next morning.

Fatima could hardly get her food down, but bite by bite she forced herself, to avoid making Ilham suspicious.

A little while later Ilham entered with Basil and Reem and picked up the tray. Basil and Reem embraced Fatima and Ilham left.

Basil called after her down the corridor, "I will soon join you, Ilham." Then he closed the door. Basil turned to Fatima and explained that their plans had changed. They were no longer going to Khartoum Airport, as it was considered too risky; someone might recognize them there. Instead, they would travel north by car to Atbara, where they would meet a caravan arranged by Basil. It would bring them to Wadi Hafa and over the border to Egypt. Then by boat up the never-ending Nile. Basil's voice was warm and his eyes serious. Fatima had always been in love with Basil's beautiful eyes, but she was unnerved by Basil's suppressed agitation.

He realized and gave her a gentle hug. "Now cousin, just be your feisty self. Everything is planned to the minutest detail. Your passport is ready—you just have to sign it. You'll be fine. I will get you safely out of here."

Basil had spent a year in New York after earning his medical degree in Khartoum. This had Americanized him, as some family members would claim. His attitudes were modern; Fatima knew she could trust him. She put on a brave smile.

"I know, Basil. We'll get ready." To Fatima it sounded like they were now speaking the words of a theatre script.

Basil turned towards his sister. "And you, Reem. Keep your cool. There may be a lot of screaming and yelling tomorrow—as we talked about. Just stay focused on our goal, saving Fatima." He looked encouraging at his sister, "I know, I can rely on you," he said and gave her a quick embrace before he left the room.

As soon as he had closed the door, Fatima and Reem began to undress. They didn't look at each other. As Reem handed Fatima her long top and loose pants, Fatima dropped them on the floor and they bumped their heads as they both bent forward to pick up the clothes.

Her head throbbing, Fatima still didn't look into Reem's face but kept her glance down while she tried to get her leg into the pants. Her body shook so much that she kept missing the pant leg. Reem had to steady her and support her to get dressed. Then Reem tumbled into Fatima's skirt and blouse.

Fatima's mind had gone blank. She couldn't think. Events had simply taken over.

Reem pointed to the angereeb and Fatima sat down; Reem undid her braids by the temple and brushed her hair loose. Afterwards Reem quickly braided some strands of hair on both sides of her own face. They stood out in awkward angles but she would have to fix them later. All the while they were silent, breathing in short puffs. Orange jumped up between them and they finally looked at each other and both broke into nervous laughter. What a sight they must be. What wouldn't Afraa say?

Reem handed her tobe to Fatima, then she got up and walked over to a large canvas bag. "Here's my bag. It's for your toiletries and your diary and whatever." Reem emptied out her stuff and Fatima looked for her own little handbag under her bed.

What could she put in the canvas bag? Fatima thought. How could one fit a whole life into one canvas bag?

Fatima's mouth was completely dry. She straightened up and looked at her cousin and best friend as she started to wrap the tobe on top of the shirt and pants. "Reem, will you be okay?"

"Sure. Nobody will know till tomorrow the earliest, and you will already be far up north. Basil told me they would not take the normal route with the caravan in case the uncles set after you."

"I didn't ask if I would be okay, but if you would be."

"I'll be fine. You know, some of your family on your mother's side are involved in this. It's all planned. All you have to do is follow."

There it was again. Everything was arranged: she just followed.

"It's all written," Reem said reassuringly.

There was that fatalism again. Reem meant well but she had said the wrong thing. Fatima froze.

There was a rapid knocking on the door that Fatima didn't recognize. Basil entered.

"Are you ready?" he whispered. "Ilham is busy in the kitchen with some fūl for tomorrow. Now is a good moment."

Reem picked up Orange.

Fatima looked down.

"Okay," Basil reached out his arm towards Fatima.

Head down-turned, Fatima didn't move.

"I'll take good care of Orange," Reem whispered.

Fatima took a step backwards. She heard herself say, "No, I'm not."

"Hurry up, we must leave immediately," Basil said urgently.

"No."

"What?"

"I am not going," Fatima said, her voice trembling. "I have made the decision not to go."

Basil looked at Fatima incredulously. "You're just too nervous now. Everything will be fine."

Fatima stood, silent.

"The car is right out there. All you have to do is walk out the door and get in. And Amel, your favorite aunt, is there in the back seat waiting for you. You can lean back and we'll take care of you."

A wave of doubt clouded Fatima's features. A little older than Fatima, Amel had always been a model for her.

"No."

"Come," Reem whispered, pulling Fatima by her arm.

Fatima thought of her uncle, his sad looks. The faces of her sisters and Reem and grandmother merged into a blur. Even Ilham. "No, I'm not coming. I have made up my mind. I am staying."

"Come, old scaredy-cat."

This time Reem's taunt made Fatima stronger. She stopped thinking of her family; instead she focused on the old banyan tree, roots dug deep into the ground. "Sorry, Reem. I hate to disappoint you. I'm not a scaredy-cat. This is my decision."

"You're losing it," Basil said loudly.

"No, I'm not losing it," Fatima said even louder.

"Have you gone out of your mind?" Basil shouted.

"No," Fatima repeated. "No, no, no," she yelled as Basil pulled her forcefully toward the door.

Ilham rushed in. "Yani, What's going on?"

"Well, we had a disagreement," Basil said, quieting his voice.

"We have to leave, Reem." Basil pulled Fatima further toward the door, but she now clung to Ilham's skirt.

"I am Fatima," Fatima said emphatically while Ilham stared, open-mouthed.

Basil took the kitten out of Reem's arms and threw it on the angereeb. He grabbed his sister's sleeve and pulled her quickly out the door.

Ilham put her arms around the sobbing Fatima. Outside, the car roared into life. The tires screeched against the gravel and the sound of the engine disappeared into the distance.

Ilham kept her arms tightly around Fatima. "Allah Karim. Allah is merciful. "

fourteen

"Allah Akbar. Allah is Great." Fatima heard the muezzin calling for prayer in the distance. Was she actually in Cairo, or was it just a dream? It was still pitch dark outside but the sounds of the town in prayer promised a speedy end to the long night. Just then Orange meowed and jumped onto her angereeb. "Al ham de l'Allah, thanks to Allah," she whispered and cuddled Orange. She was still home. She jumped out of her bed and kneeled for her morning prayer as Ilham entered with some karkade.

Ilham waited till Fatima had finished her prayer. Then she said, "I had a message from your grandmother's house. She has returned safely, Al' ham de l'Allah, and intends to come and see you today."

"Grandmother," Fatima shouted in joy. "I knew you would come. I knew." She grabbed Ilham and swung her around. Ilham turned a round or two before she disengaged herself. She smiled and patted Fatima on her cheek.

"She will visit around noon. But I have work to do. Soon it will be Eid," and Ilham hurried out the door.

Fatima looked after her in wonder. Not a word about yesterday. As if it hadn't happened. As if Ilham had seen nothing.

Fatima was standing in the middle of her room. She took

a step towards her angereeb, then she turned and walked through her outside door. She inhaled the fresh morning air. She could have been far away from here. Basil and Amel were probably on their way to Egypt now. Or maybe they hadn't left after Fatima changed her mind. But Ilham's lips were sealed—that much Fatima knew.

"Grandmother, dear grandmother, you're coming," Fatima said aloud. The next hours would seem very long and she was too agitated to write. She decided to take a bath and get herself ready for their meeting and Fatima headed towards the corridor door. But before she reached it she stopped. She couldn't believe she had decided against escaping; on the other hand, she always wanted to stay right here in Sudan. She wanted to become a teacher like Amel, and she wanted to change many of the harmful traditions. She wanted Sudan to be the wonderful place it really was.

Fatima was still standing in the middle of the floor. Slowly she walked back to her angereeb and sat down. Surely this could only be if her grandmother and uncle succeeded in settling. She believed they would; they knew the people they dealt with. She would pray to Allah.

Fatima went to her little bathroom to fetch water. Back in her room, she took off Reem's clothes and folded them carefully before she bathed both herself and Orange in the cool water. She didn't notice it wasn't warm. She put on her prettiest blouse and long skirt, and found a ribbon for Orange. She sat waiting while the heat built up in her room. The air turned heavy, thunder was coming.

Finally, Fatima heard the irregular walk with the familiar tap of the walking stick. The door opened with no knocking and there she appeared her grandmother—a little unsteady—with lifted arms to embrace Fatima. Fatima buried her head in the grandmother's soft front-side. Tears running down her cheeks, she wanted to stand like that forever, but after a little while her grandmother relieved her embrace gently but firmly.

Fatima made her grandmother sit down on her only chair and the old lady stretched her hand toward the glass and water carafe. She took a little sip. Her grandmother was too old for fasting; she didn't eat, but she would drink a little water. She dabbed her forehead with a small white handkerchief. Fatima smelled the familiar sandal wood from the scented cloth. The aroma pulled her into the familiar sphere of security and comfort that surrounded her grandmother.

Her grandmother kept dabbing her forehead and stretched out her trunk-like legs. She loosened her verdigris green tobe from her knotty arms to get a little more air. Fatima thought she looked more and more like the old banyan tree in her garden, weathered by many sunny days and storms.

"So, how are you holding up?"

"I don't know, Grandmother. I was praying every day for you to return. I was waiting for you. I had planned with Aunt Selma and Reem and Basil to flee the country. But then I didn't want to leave." Fatima's tears were streaming again.

"They are still here."

"Who?"

"Basil and Amel."

"But I thought Basil wanted to go to America?"

"Yes, but not without you."

"But?"

"He can still leave."

Her grandmother was perspiring. "We need to talk about you. What are your plans? What do you expect to do now that you decided to stay in Sudan?"

"I want to finish my college and become a teacher."

"You cannot stay in Khartoum so your college is out. Teacher maybe." Her grandmother looked at her like from far away. "We must take you away from Khartoum. Your uncles will want that. And you would be ostracized to a great extent here." Her grandmother stuck to the subject.

"But where can I go?" Fatima asked humbly. She realized she was dependent on her grandmother—at least for now.

The grandmother's furrowed face lit up. "I could take you to our relatives in the village in Darfur. I was just there and know they would take you in."

"But what will I do far away from my family and Khartoum?" Fatima asked sadly.

"That's the whole point, you could teach there—as you wish to. I have plans for starting a primary school there. The village people are keen. You have the qualifications and I have the influence and some money to get the project started. You will work and do something good for yourself and society."

The grandmother took another small sip of water. "Then it will be up to you to succeed," she added.

Fatima was dumbfounded. "I would love to do that. That was my secret dream."

Fatima went over to the grandmother and put her arms around her. "Grandmother you give me a new life."

"But this is only if we make a settlement. Uncle Moham-mad will not let you go for nothing; he will want his blood money."

"But how can we get enough money together?" Fatima asked. Then her face brightened, "I could pay him out of my salary. For years to come. It would be right that I must pay."

"Oh, sweetie. I think you're a little too optimistic. I don't believe that would be enough. I had a conversation with your father's oldest brother on the phone and I am going to meet him and the two other brothers in the afternoon. I have a plan."

"I knew you would," Fatima said with a sad smile.

"Yes, but I don't know if it will work, although I have reasons to believe it will." The grandmother kept patting her forehead with the kerchief.

Fatima inhaled the sandalwood scent.

"I just knew you would," Fatima repeated.

"Don't count your chickens before they hatch." The grand-mother smiled, she didn't mind her granddaughter believed in her. "My plan is quite simple. As I don't have a tremen-dous lot of money, I will offer my house with the large gar-den in *diya*, blood money, to your oldest uncle."

"Oh, no, you can't do that," Fatima exclaimed.

"So you would rather give your life?" the grandmother said curtly. "Don't be silly. I happen to know that your pater-nal Uncle Muhammad has made some money transactions that went sour. Your uncle is in a bad spot, although this is not known publicly. He recently made an extremely advan-tageous marriage arrangement for his oldest son with the daughter of the minister of commerce and is in dire need of a house for the couple. My house would solve his problems and enable your uncle to hide his bad economic circumstances. The marriage would give him connections high up, bringing new opportunities for him. You know how ambitious and greedy he is. You have to know your puppets," the grandmother concluded.

"Our beloved house. My banyan tree," Fatima said mournfully.

"But if we don't make a settlement; we'll have to sneak you out of here immediately. That's why Basil stayed behind. He will have to get you out of Sudan the very same day. There will be no time to lose."

"Oh, no," Fatima yelled.

"Yani. That is, maybe your banyan tree will perform the magic," the grandmother said soothingly. "But I don't have time to sit here babbling any longer. I must be off. I am going straight to your paternal uncle's house. Say your prayers."

With difficulty, the grandmother got up from her chair and began to wrap the tobe over her head and shoulders and arms till only her face was uncovered.

"But where will you stay, grandma, if you have no house?"
"I will find out. Maybe aunt Selma. She already asked me to come live with her. She didn't think I should live in that large house alone. So you see: everything can be arranged."

"Ah, grandma."

Fatima noticed that her grandmother's eyes were moist when she gave Fatima a quick embrace and walked towards the door in her rocking way. "And in this heat," she sighed as she opened the door.

Alone in the room after the grandmother had left, Fatima heard another roll of thunder as she paced. She looked out her window but there were no clouds, even though the air felt sultry. How strange life was: they would settle and she would resume her life in a village—perhaps the kind of village Ilham left ten years ago? But Fatima would be teaching.

Fatima picked up the Koran and read the line about education. She turned the leaves to the section about women. It was easy to find, as the pages were a little smudgy and worn. There it was: "….and clothe them and give them a good education." Very brief. If only Prophet Mohammad had reported more about the subject. And Fatima didn't like that it was up to the men to do this; it shouldn't be benevolence; it should be a right for both boys and girls.

But the Koran was positive. Then it would be up to her to create the content of this education—that was the challenge. Slowly Fatima got up from her bed and sat down to write. No more thunder; the storm must have gone elsewhere. She moved her hands slowly and purposelessly; she felt a growing energy.

It would be up to her, Fatima, to succeed.

fifteen

18 January B'ism'illah.

Finally, finally my grandmother came. And she had a plan like I thought she would. She understood I wanted to teach. I have to admit that the plans are mostly hers but then I will be able to take over and make it mine. It gives me great hope and happiness.

Only I cannot be sure her house will be accepted by my uncles. Especially Uncle Hamid, since it goes to Uncle Muhammad. Deep down I have a fear. The most terrible thing could happen—so I just cannot even think that.

I pray to Allah to let me live so I can redeem myself.

After her evening meal Fatima rested on her angereeb, her shawl loosely over her, when Ilham's familiar steps came down the corridor. Ilham knocked and entered. "Eid Mubarak. Happy Eid. The moon has been spotted. Tomorrow we'll celebrate Eid al-Fitr. Festival of breaking the fast." Fatima embraced Ilham. "Your uncle is back. He will meet your other uncles and your grandmother. They will come tomorrow morning."

Ilham handed Fatima a small box. "Here, open this. It is from your uncle."

Hesitantly Fatima took the box and opened the lid. Inside were little square pieces of chocolate, already beginning to melt in the heat.

"Thank you, thank you. But why should my uncle send me chocolate?"

"Because of the holiday Eid."

Fatima looked at Ilham. Why would they give her chocolate? Did Ilham know something? Was she just covering up with her cheerful façade? Suddenly Fatima was gripped by the most profound fear. She was going to die. She was going to die. How could she have fooled herself for so long? She could hardly breathe. The walls were closing in on her. She cried out in fear, and Ilham grabbed her and held her tightly while she screamed and screamed.

Slowly her screams turned into sobbing while Ilham patted her back. "B'ism'illah. In the name of God."

"Don't leave me, Ilham. I don't want to be alone."

"I will stay. I will stay." And Ilham struck Fatima softly till she finally calmed down, with only an occasional sob.

"What happened to your little braids?" Ilham whispered and went to the far end of the room to retrieve Fatima's brush.

She sat down on the angereeb next to Fatima and gently brushed out her tangled hair. Then she divided three strands of hair on one temple and braided them deftly. She hummed a little tune Fatima knew from her grandmother. She went over to the other side of Fatima and braided that side, too. Fatima's last sob turned into a sighing yawn.

"Please stay with me tonight, Ilham."

Fatima didn't stir when late in the night Ilham tiptoed out of the room.

On the table the pieces of chocolate had melted into little sad mounds, a ghostly almond on top.

The sun was already warming the right side of the wall when Fatima woke up. It was late. Ilham had opened the shutters, but she hadn't come with the karkade as usual. Ah, it was Eid. Her fast was over. Everyone's fast was over. Ilham had let her sleep in. Fatima remained still for a while, Orange curled up by her feet. Then she remembered her panic last night. But she felt so peaceful now listening to the chirping birds.

She loved the fresh, quiet mornings. She loved Sudan. She surely didn't want to be a rootless immigrant in America. But would she be safe if she stayed? Her uncles and their sons—and maybe some of the women too—might resort to honor killing? She had caused the death of her father and to them it was a spot on the family name. Fatima shook her head. How could you "erase" a killing by by killing another family member? How could killing restore your family dignity? Didn't it just add a new crime to the old one? How could her death satisfy Hamid's sons? Now she remembered how she had once overheard her mother say to her father in the other room, "Those Hamid boys are up to no good roaming the streets instead of studying." And now one of them had turned "religious," Fatima had heard. She shuddered.

Fatima got up and began to pace her tile floor. Her recent nightmare crushed over her like a giant wave.

She needed to calm down.

Fatima walked outside. The jacaranda was a cacophony of blues and purples wrapped in the sound of humming bees. She felt the warm rays on her skin. She lifted up her face and soaked up the sunbeams. She felt she was like the young, blooming jacaranda tree. Then she turned back towards the door and discovered the ephemeral curved sliver of the new moon above the house. It looked like a tiny cradle. She walked in and closed the screen door behind her.

Reassured, she took the pencil in her hand and began to write. She wanted to explain how her long Ramadan month had changed her. On and on she went.

She felt so grateful. She sat for a while with the end of the pencil in her mouth. There was a tiny piece of eraser at the very end of a rim of ribbed metal. The metal had a slightly bitter taste. She erased the last lines up to the date 19 January 1999. Then she added, *I am waiting to be born*, before she gently closed her diary.

All she could do now was to wait.

But it was like the morning would never end. Like time had stopped. Fatima stretched out on her angereeb. She thought of how her whole life had been one long waiting as a little girl not allowed to go outside in their garden till her older sister came home; waiting to be old enough to go to school with other girls; waiting for her aunt Selma and cousin Reem to come by; even waiting and dreading her circumcision; waiting to grow up so she could go to college like Zena and drive through town in the minivan and crossing the river on her way to the Women's College in Omdurman. Zena had whispered to her about it when they had been made to go to bed early waiting for sleep to relieve them. Even—deep down—waiting to get married one day so she could leave the house of her parents. Waiting, waiting always. Looking through the window at the palm tree gently swaying in the breeze outside. Outside. On the other side of the window. Just like now, confined to her room. Waiting and not even knowing what she was waiting for.

Time could stand still, which it mostly did; and then it could suddenly accelerate.

There was a knock on the door that she didn't recognize. It opened before she could answer and Basil appeared putting his finger to his lips. "Shush, shush. Don't be afraid but I have to speak quickly; we don't have much time. Sorry, if I got a little excited yesterday but your life is at risk. That's why I am back. So straight to the point. Fatima, will you come with me right now? This very moment?"

Fatima emitted a small scream of surprise.

"Shush. I don't think you're safe—you have to get out of here."

"But grandma is trying to settle."

"I know and there is a good chance she will succeed—but if she doesn't there may not be enough time to get you out unnoticed. Our uncles may take you away immediately."

"Oh," Fatima screamed. She started to cry and Basil put his arm protectively around her.

"But I think she will settle," Basil said soothingly.

Fatima had put her face on Basil's chest. Basil padded her patiently on her back. After a while her sobbing abated and she said quietly, "Yes, maybe she will settle. May be I can stay and go to Darfur and teach."

"Darfur?"

"Yes, we talked about that. Grandma...."

"Grandma was always very optimistic and I don't know about Darfur? But there is another point. If we make a settlement it may work for the older generation."

"What do you mean?"

"Nothing specific but I don't trust some of our family. Those younger hot heads. They are already talking about family honor."

Fatima didn't know what to say and put her head back against Basil's chest.

"How about Uncle Hamid and his sons?"

"Exactly. They have already been making noises—and if grandma's house goes to Muhammad, Uncle Hamid may not be satisfied even if Uncle Muhammad offers to reimburse him."

"Your life may be in danger and I care too much about you, Fatima, not to try to save you."

Basil looked at her with those brown eyes of his. Fatima hesitated. She didn't know what to say when they both turned their heads towards the screen door. They heard a car had stopped outside the gate and soon after the light blue gate rattled and the inside handle moved as somebody was trying to turn the handle on the street side.

"Damn it. They are already here," Basil said. "And they are coming to the back gate instead of the front one."

Slowly the heavy gate opened and separated. Both metal doors trembled as they were pushed inwards against lawn and gravel. Through the filter of the screen Fatima glimpsed the dark blue suits of her uncles—even her maternal uncle was wearing a navy suit. As she looked at the bluish blur, it seemed to split at the center and the grandmother's bright tobe, with green leaves on sandy brown, emerged; a banyan tree with the Nile in the background.

"Quick, quick, we have to escape through the house and the front gate." Basil grabbed Fatima's hand and pulled her towards the inside door.

"Come with me."

Fatima looked at Basil and then back at the emerging family. It was now she would have to make her own decision. This very second.

EPILOGUE

GENESIS

Fatima's Room has been long in coming and it has undergone many a metamorphosis from its initial interview form, via first person diary, to finally, fictional novel. Its origin dates back to when I lived in Sudan and taught English and Women's Studies at the Ahfad University for Women in 1991–1993. I also lived in Khartoum in 1985–1987 but it was my contact with the young female students—and not all so young female teachers—that the material for my novel was fostered through my interviews with more than twenty women. The students would seek me out as a sounding board and confidante after classes. I learned more and more about their lives and thoughts and was surprised at how open they were, even about their experiences with the dreaded female genital mutilation. It occurred to me that I could conduct interviews with a small cassette recorder around the issues they brought up the most.

My group came from the educated women in the capital and I was especially interested in how these women found themselves trapped between their traditional culture and the growing influence of Western, and individualistic, ideas. They lived in an environment of great restrictions on women, sexually segregated, and they aspired for more freedom and opportunity without necessarily rejecting all the traditional values and especially not their religion. Most were Muslim but there were also Christians from the South. (This was before the South became independent.)

When I returned to Berkeley, California, I went through the arduous work of transcribing the texts. It was slow work and I hired some students to help me with the job. But what could I do with the interviews? I wanted to publish them. But how? They would need a context. My academic background (Scandinavian Literature and Languages) pointed to the scholarly route. I borrowed all the relevant books on Sudan I could find in the Doe Library on campus. They had it all; and I proceeded to write a lengthy introduction outlining the history, religion, and culture of Sudan, followed by a summary of women in the Arab world to finally focus on women in the Sudan.

My introduction grew and the bibliography extended over four pages. I realized the interviews were too long, uneven, and repetitious. I decided to take selections from the interviews that could illustrate the points made in the introduction. Thus "the founding mother" of *Fatima's Room* came into being as Voices in the Making: Sudanese Women Speak. It consisted of 37 pages of introduction; 2 pages footnotes; 4 pages bibliography; and 50 pages selections from interviews. I bought *The Writers Market* and started looking for academic presses. I sent my manuscript to about thirteen academic presses, which all returned the manuscript but not without many an encouraging and appreciative comment. I think I came close but that was, of course, not enough.

Then I received a letter from The Feminist Press in New York; they were interested. I didn't hear from them for a long time and almost forgot about them when I finally got the courage to call them up. They had run out of money; they were very apologetic. I still couldn't let go and decided instead to write a fictional story based on the material from the interviews. It became a story about a Sudanese woman, who kills her father, in first person diary form. I called it Dear Mom; the student whom the story is the closest to called me "Mom." So it was like her writing to me.

But I hadn't really found my narrative form and tone. An editor, whom I found through a contact, kindly turned it down. She found the content interesting but she didn't think the quality of the writing measured up. She advised me to work harder on my writing skills and used Wallace Wegner as an example. Could Wallace Wegner show me the way? Maybe. But for now I put my manuscript in the bottom of the drawer.

It was not till we went to Ethiopia in 2000–2002 for two years and I began to write Stories from Ethiopia—historical and contemporary short stories—that my writing skills began to improve. Finally, back in Berkeley and during summers in our cottage on the Danish island of Ærø, I began to write most mornings. One day I pulled Dear Mom out of hiding and started on it afresh with Fatima as a central, fictional character.

FACT AND FICTION

The story of Fatima is from one of my students, whose name was not Fatima. She had told me about herself and her five sisters and their unhappy home life, where the girls functioned as domestics and were denied any recognition as an individual person. She related how the father always shouted to them, "I will kill you if... you don't come straight home from school. I will kill you if... this. ...if... that." What if SHE killed HIM? That story has never been told. A daughter who kills her father is not possible. Her husband, yes. Her children, yes. But her father? No. It appealed to me because it symbolizes the ultimate rebellion against patriarchal suppression.

This became the germ of my fictional story in which I had to choose and shape settings to support and move the story forward. I finally could use all the material I had from the interviews; I just had to fit it into my story. I also could draw from the extensive reading I had done about women and Sudan, as in the zar scene and the traditional wedding dance.

Clearly genital mutilation was one of the prominent subjects from the interviews so I have Fatima experience it, talk about it, and think about it. As happens when you create a character that character begins to take on a life of her own. I had not imagined that I would make Fatima sexually active (especially under her particular circumstances) but it came from Fatima; it was a consequence of her seclusion but also a sense of freedom and privacy—something she had not enjoyed before. And her growing awareness of intimacy led her to greater understanding of sexuality and society. She now connected the dots between her mutilation, her sexual pleasure, and social suppression. That new insight helped give her a sense of identity and purpose.

I have retained the diary idea from *Dear Mom* in a reduced form to underscore how Fatima is on a quest to find herself;

who she is; what her life means. Maybe that's why I decided to let the entire novel take place in a room of her own so-to-speak. I came to like the idea of Fatima imprisoned in a room. I wanted to stay close to Fatima as the center of conflicts and emotions. I also liked the dramatic juxtapositions of her and her various visitors, which this setting offered, rendering the story theatrical and providing a seemingly simple structure to complex issues.

FATIMA AND HER READER

Although my interviews are now over twenty years old, major parts of the world have not changed fundamentally with regard to the suppression of women. Female genital mutilation is still common and honor-killings still take place to mention just two major subjects. The underlying issue of traditional society versus modernity and respect for the individual is, in fact, a burning issue across the world. One that has developed into armed conflict, with unheard of antagonism as with the Taliban in Afghanistan. We need to understand these issues from inside as Fatima is beginning to do. Fatima does not reject her Muslim faith; on the contrary, it is very important to her. But she does question how it deals with women in the present world. Why can't there be progressive changes so women can feel comfortable with their faith in a modern more equal world?

This novel is set in the Muslim world, but the question of modernity and tradition is relevant throughout the world. Here in the United States the discussion also often hinges on whether to take the Constitution (like the Koran) literally or according to implied intention enabling adaptation for modern times. Although in different forms, the Western world shares similar fundamental issues. The Western woman is also struggling for more freedom, equality, and respect.

Finally, I want to address the issue of why I, a "white woman," wrote about a part of the world that is not mine. It is true, I moved back to my "own" world after living in the Sudan, Yemen, India, and Ethiopia for close to fifteen years, long enough to know these cultures well and to make friendships of love and solidarity. So what I experienced so deeply there, it's not of "them" and "us." It is of all women in the global world of 2017. It is of our world.

ABOUT THE AUTHOR

Charlotte Schiander Gray was born in Copenhagen in 1944. After earning her PhD in Scandinavian Languages and Literature at the University of California at Berkeley, she accompanied her husband to Yemen. In Sudan she taught English and Women's Studies at the Ahfad University for Women in 1991–1993, and also lived in Khartoum from 1985–1987. She published academic articles and book reviews on Scandinavian literature, and wrote a book on the Danish author Klaus Rifbjerg.

Returning to California, Charlotte taught literature at UC Berkeley Extension and volunteered for the Friends of the Berkeley Public Library, while raising three sons. For the past fifteen years she has also written fictional stories of her life in foreign countries, and spends the summer months in her second home on the Danish island of Ærø.